THREE
SILVER
DOVES

A Paige MacKenzie Mystery

Deborah Garner

Cranberry Cove Press

Three Silver Doves
by Deborah Garner

First Printing – June 2015
ISBN: 978-0-9960449-3-6

Printed in the U.S.A.

Also by Deborah Garner

Above the Bridge
The Moonglow Café
Cranberry Bluff

To Elizabeth Christy

CHAPTER ONE

Gravel shot up against the underside of Paige's car as she navigated the steep, dusty road. She pressed her foot against the brake pedal to slow the momentum of the vehicle as it responded to the downward incline.

The sharp upward grade of the road had been unsettling enough as she ascended the Sangre de Christo mountain range. But the downhill portion was proving even more challenging. Between the gravity pulling her rented Camry forward and the staccato pings of stones against metal, her nerves were on edge.

Tall, ponderosa pines cast late afternoon shadows, adding a surreal element to an already eerie journey. She glanced at her odometer: two more miles. She exhaled slowly, both an attempt to relax and a sigh of relief. She was almost at her destination.

Agua Encantada nestled into a small valley, set against a backdrop of granite slabs that soared skyward with an alarming sense of permanence and power. By comparison, the reclusive hot springs resort appeared as tiny and fragile as a bird's nest. Fragile, Paige thought as she swerved to avoid a pothole – exactly the way she felt after four months of New York winter.

She rolled the car window down, but quickly rolled it back up as dust slapped the side of her face. The fresh New Mexico air waited on the valley floor, and she was looking forward to clearing out her lungs. After she returned to New York from her two previous trips – one to Jackson Hole, Wyoming, the other to Timberton, Montana – she'd been unable to get re-acclimated to city air quality. By assigning her a series of articles on the Old West, *The Manhattan Post* had inadvertently given her a gift. She'd found a different way of life – one that included not only clean air, but the camaraderie of small town residents.

As always before heading out on an assignment, Paige had done her research on Agua Encantada. The resort dated back centuries. Long before the mineral pools were developed and the guest casitas built, rumors of the water's healing powers had drawn those seeking rejuvenation and health. Legend had it that young children had been cured of polio and that the elderly had found freedom from respiratory distress. Paige hoped the water would vanquish her own blues, which had grown worse as the East Coast winter dragged on. When her editor, Susan, had suggested an article on southwestern hot springs for an upcoming special issue on health, Paige had jumped at the suggestion.

Everything Paige had ever heard or read about the Southwest had intrigued her. Descriptions of warm colors, soft breezes and savory spices beckoned her with the promise of hospitality. As she pulled up in front of the small, adobe office, she was beginning to have second thoughts. The property looked sparse and deserted, and the sunshine that had accompanied her from Albuquerque's airport was quickly slipping behind ominous clouds. Shadows, previously cast by local landscape, faded into nothingness. A gust of wind sent a flurry of dust across the hood of her car.

Paige set the emergency brake and pulled the keys from the ignition, pausing only long enough to take a deep breath and let out an exhausted sigh. Travel fatigue often skewed her first impressions of destinations, so she tried not to take them too seriously. A hot shower and a good meal would help, the sooner the better, she thought as she stepped out of the car.

The wind whipped her shoulder-length hair to the side and pressed her faded T-shirt against her slender body as she approached the building. The office door's warped screen shuddered within its frame, threatening to tear loose from the thick, mustard-colored adobe brick. Paige grasped the handle and pulled the door open, stepping inside. She closed the screen door behind her and looked around.

Decorated in warm, soothing colors, the lobby was a welcome relief from the chilly weather outside. Thick Navajo rugs in reds and grays covered the floors, and bright paintings of southwestern landscapes hung on the walls above leather couches and armchairs. A kiva fireplace filled a far corner of the room, flanked by fireplace tools and buckets of wood. A display case to the left of a registration counter exhibited Native American wares. Stepping closer, Paige peered inside, taking in varied pottery, silver jewelry and carved stone figurines. She'd seen similar carvings before and knew them to be Zuni fetishes, but the variety surprised her: bears and horses, as well as badgers, rabbits, snakes, coyotes and birds – some smaller, some larger and all intricately carved. Small cards rested alongside each figure, naming the artist, animal and type of stone.

"Beautiful, aren't they?"

Paige turned to the counter as a woman in her early twenties greeted her. The woman's hair, almost black, was drawn back and held at the nape of her neck with an intricately designed barrette of silver and turquoise. Matching earrings dangled above a ruffled white blouse with embroidered flowers around the neckline. Dark brown eyes hovered below lush eyelashes.

"Yes, they are," Paige said. "Zuni fetishes, right?" She glanced back at the case, noticing a deep blue figure of a mammal of some sort. Squinting, she tried to make out the animal – a mountain lion, perhaps?

"Yes. They're from my mother's store – it's called Luz, just like her name," the young woman said. "It's in our town, Tres Palomas. You'll have to visit it while you're here."

"I would love to." Paige faced the counter again. "Tres Palomas...that means three doves, right?

"Very good. Do you speak Spanish?"

"Barely any," Paige admitted. "*Un poquito.*" She held up one hand, thumb and index finger barely spread apart.

"Ah, just a little." The woman nodded.

"Is Tres Palomas far from here?"

"A few miles, only. An easy drive. There's a little bar and café there called the Coyote Cantina – a hole in the wall, but popular with locals. And a beautiful, old adobe church. And, of course, my mother's store."

The young woman smiled, revealing a row of natural white teeth, set off against a deep tan. Not a single wrinkle broke the smooth surface of her skin. "You must be Paige MacKenzie," she said, sliding a registration card across the counter. "Welcome to Agua Encantada – 'Enchanted Water.' Since you're the only guest checking in today, I knew who you were as soon as your car pulled up. I'm Marisol. My mother runs the resort when she's not at her store, but I'm usually the one manning the desk. How was your trip?"

"Uneventful but long," Paige admitted. "Between the two-hour layover in Dallas and the drive up from

Albuquerque, I've been traveling for about ten hours." She pulled her cell phone out of one pocket to check the time.

"The time difference makes it harder, too," Marisol said. "You'll be hungry soon, I imagine. Our café is not offering dinner tonight, but will be open tomorrow at breakfast. We serve a simple meal each morning, whether we have guests or not, so the staff can eat." She gestured to a door beside the kiva fireplace. A sign above the door announced the back room as simply "Café."

"I can give you suggestions for tonight," Marisol continued, "the easiest being homemade tamales. I just made them yesterday. It'll save you the drive into Tres Palomas."

A sharp crackle of thunder outside made it an easy decision. A downpour of rain was imminent and the driveway had been difficult enough to navigate when dry. "Homemade tamales would be wonderful," Paige said. She filled out the registration card and handed it back to Marisol.

"You're in the Garden Casita," Marisol said, indicating its location on a printed map of the property. "Back toward the end of the main building, across from the spa. You'll see a parking space next to it. If you hurry, you'll make it in before the rain." She handed Paige a key, attached to a circular web of string and feathers.

"A dream catcher," Paige said, taking the key and smiling.

"Yes, right again," Marisol laughed. "Zuni fetishes and dream catchers. Maybe you've visited the Southwest before?"

"Just pre-trip research," Paige said. "I've never seen this part of the country. I've been looking forward to it."

"This is a fascinating area," Marisol said, as Paige moved toward the door. "I'm sure you'll enjoy your visit."

"I'm sure I will, too," Paige said before exiting the office and heading for the casita.

* * * *

The dream catcher swayed as increasingly forceful gusts of wind sent the circular web of feathers and beads into motion. Paige slipped the key into the door of the Garden Casita. The small studio was as welcoming as the lobby: golden-yellow paint on the adobe walls, a kiva fireplace in one corner that promised additional warmth in the evenings. The comforter on the double bed featured angular, brick red shapes with sienna Kokopelli figures spread throughout the design. Two bedside tables held reading lamps with tin shades. One window, not more than two feet across, was embedded into one of the walls. On a non-stormy day, it would throw more light across the room than the current gray clouds allowed. Conveniently, a writing desk rested below it. The cozy armchair by the fireplace looked the most inviting, bringing an image of evening reading to mind. After all, she had promised herself equal parts writing and relaxation on this trip.

Paige turned to an alcove near the door, setting her luggage on a low wooden bench below a half dozen dangling hangers. She crossed the room to a small bathroom where she twisted the faucet handle, leaned over the basin, and splashed cold water on her face. Looking up, she hardly recognized herself in the tin-framed mirror. Her green eyes, normally bright, looked almost gray, and her auburn hair drooped around her face, dull and lifeless. Her muscles ached. The drive from Albuquerque had unnerved and exhausted her. Suddenly the bed in the main room seemed especially inviting – that or one of the mineral pools she'd read so much about.

A flash of lightning eliminated the idea of soaking in an outdoor pool. She'd hope for sunshine the next day and spend the evening unpacking and settling in.

Pulling her cell phone out, she was discouraged to find no service. She'd told Jake about the trip and wanted at least to let him know she'd arrived safely, but calling him would have to wait.

Paige took toiletries from her overnight bag and set them on the bathroom counter, admiring the bright mosaic of blue and red tiling. As she headed back to the main room to pull clothing from her suitcase, she heard a knock at the door.

Strong wind pushed the door inward as Paige opened it. As expected, Marisol stood on the doorstep, a foil-covered plate in her hands.

"*Tamales, senorita*," Marisol said as she handed the plate to Paige. She shivered visibly as another burst of wind swept in. "There are two kinds, beef and chicken. The beef has red chili in it and the chicken has *salsa verde*. Both are delicious. I put some sliced mango on the plate, too."

"Thank you. You should come in," Paige said, watching the first torrent of rain hit the ground behind Marisol.

"No, but thank you," Marisol said quickly. "The storm will get worse before it gets better. I should head back to the office. But enjoy the tamales. I'm glad you won't be trying to drive into town in this weather."

"That makes two of us," Paige said as the rain began to pour down harder. "I'm so grateful to you for sharing your food with me."

"It's not a problem," Marisol said. "When we make tamales, we make dozens – always plenty for us to share." Turning away to head back to the office, she paused long enough to point to a small bin in the outside hallway. "There

7

is wood for your fireplace, and you'll find matches in the desk drawer."

"Is there cell service here?" Paige held up her phone. "I can't seem to connect."

"Yes, most of the time," Marisol answered. "But it often goes out during storms. It should be back on later tonight or in the morning. And we always have a phone in the lobby that you can use."

"Thank you again," Paige said. "I just wanted to tell a friend I arrived safely. It can wait."

She closed the door and watched from the window of the casita as Marisol hastened toward the office. The strength of the downpour grew quickly above the dramatic landscape. The thunderous sound of rain against the rooftop lulled her mind into a flowing wave of thoughts, jumbled together and scattered like seashells. The trancelike state hardly matched the scene outside, where cactus stood stoic against the force of the downpour, yet the pampas grass whipped sideways under the dual assault of water and wind. Terra cotta containers of blue salvia cringed against nature's beating. Still the resilient New Mexico terrain stood firm.

Had she really just called Jake a "friend" when mentioning him to Marisol? He wasn't merely a friend. Yet he wasn't a...what was the current term...significant other? Why were these relationship labels so difficult to determine? For that matter, why were labels needed at all? This was always a dilemma when it came to including Jake in conversations with others.

This was the first western assignment she'd received that held little chance of seeing him. Not for lack of want on either her side or his, but simply because of logistics. She'd resigned herself to this before leaving New York.

Paige turned away from the window, set the covered dinner plate on the desk and peeked under the foil. As the enticing aromas of corn-based masa and chiles floated up to her, she realized she was hungrier than she'd thought. She pulled out the desk's rattan chair, sat down, separated the silverware from the cloth napkin, and started in.

CHAPTER TWO

Despite the storm raging outside, Paige had fallen into a deep sleep until a sharp bang roused her. Only half awake, she looked first to see if her notepad had fallen from her lap. Lulled by a combination of carbs and travel fatigue, she'd dozed off in the armchair beside the kiva fireplace, where she'd built a small fire after finishing off Marisol's tamales. Finding nothing on the floor, she moved to the window and looked outside, cracking it open to listen. Across the courtyard, the sound repeated itself. Dark now, it was difficult to see anything but sagebrush blowing across the property. Paige cupped her hands against the window and tried to get a better look. Was a person part of the moving shadows around the building opposite her casita?

Paige pulled on a jacket, thankful for a hood that could help keep rain and flying leaves from hitting her face. Succumbing to her tendency to let curiosity win out over common sense, she tucked the key to the casita in a pocket and stepped outside. Bracing herself against the storm, she headed across the courtyard, in the direction of the sound.

Paige approached the building cautiously, one hand firmly gripping the key in her pocket in case she needed to use it for self-defense. The thought that the tumbling brush might have been a person made her uneasy. Still, this was a

11

small New Mexico resort, not New York City. No vehicles parked nearby, and other tumbling shadows proved to be sagebrush. She was sure an unlatched window was causing the sounds. She would find the culprit and hope that pushing it closed firmly would engage an interior lock. If nothing else, it would be easier to sleep without the sharp, annoying sound that she'd heard from her casita.

A sign near the entrance identified the spa building. Windows bordered each side of the front door. She checked each one to make sure it was secured and then walked around the side of the building. A fence flanked the corner, closing off the back area. It wasn't hard to imagine that non-guests might help themselves to use of the pools after hours. The fence kept the area reserved for guests. Unfortunately, this also kept Paige from checking windows at the back of the building.

Back to the front, Paige checked the entrance, finding the door locked. Another crack told her a window somewhere was still unlatched. Paige headed around the other side of the building. A sudden burst of wind blew the hood of Paige's jacket off her head, a whistling batting against her ears. She closed her eyes to keep dust out and pulled the hood back up. She leaned forward into the wind and continued on. Several tumbleweeds flew by, which eased her worry that what she saw earlier was a human figure.

Reaching the fence on the other side of the building, Paige heard the bang again and weighed her options. The slamming would continue if the window were not secured. She glanced around. The office was now closed for the evening. There was probably a contact number on the office door for after-hour problems, but a loose window hardly seemed an emergency, and she hated to bother Marisol after a long day's work.

Paige estimated the fence to be about five feet high – tall enough to get the message across to stay out, but hardly enough to deter a grownup tomboy with many memories of tree climbing. She smiled as she thought back to a favorite tree from her childhood, a giant oak at the end of her grandfather's driveway. One low-swooping limb had been just the right shape for curling up with a good book. And, oh, how she had filled the hours and days with reading! She made a mental note to pick up a book the next day from the bookcase she'd seen in the lobby. A nice fire in the casita's fireplace and a peaceful evening of reading would make for a perfect night.

The sound of the window slamming again made her refocus. When she was a teen, chain-link fences were easy to scale. She grasped a section with both hands and inserted her foot into an opening, pulling herself up higher. A couple more upward grasps and toe insertions, and she was over the fence and on the other side, the howling wind drowning out the sound of her landing. Only a slight shortness of breath told her climbing fences had been easier fifteen years earlier.

Again she heard the slamming. Inside the fenced area now, Paige quickly found the window in question and reached up to press it closed, hoping a latch would catch. But, as she grasped the edge of the window, she suddenly heard rough, scraping sounds. *A chair being moved? Drawers opening and closing?* Though almost impossible to identify with the rush of wind around her ears, she was certain of one thing: someone was inside.

Instead of closing the window, Paige held it open and attempted to look inside, but even standing on tiptoe, she was not eye-level with the windowsill. She tried a quiet jump, light enough for the wind to cover the sound of her landing. It was no use, even when she repeated the process. She paused, hearing the same noises from within, then gave it one more try, pushing higher off the ground. Clumsily, she touched down on a rock just uneven enough to cause her to lose her balance. As she fell, her head tapped a vertical rain gutter with a dull, metal thud. She held her breath as the sounds inside ceased.

Frozen, Paige listened as footsteps filled the silence followed by the sound of a door opening and closing. She drew herself up off the ground and moved along the wall, crouching behind shrubbery as the footsteps resumed, this time outdoors, coming closer. They stopped near the fence she had scaled. A flashlight switched on and roamed the grounds, passing dangerously close to her hiding spot. *A security guard? A burglar?* She remained still, her heart pounding. *You haven't even been here twenty-four hours and you're already in trouble.*

Several minutes passed before the flashlight turned off and the steps faded, long enough for Paige to wrack her brain for excuses, should she be discovered. *I was just trying to close the window. I didn't want to disturb the office.* Any way she looked at it, she was still guilty of entering a fenced-off area.

She waited long enough to be certain she was alone again and then quickly scaled the fence and returned to her casita. Once inside, she fell back against the door and took a deep breath, exhaling slowly. In spite of feeling relieved, she couldn't fend off a nagging thought, even as she finally undressed and slipped into bed. *Who had been inside the spa building? And why?*

CHAPTER THREE

Sunshine streamed in through the casita window as Paige opened her eyes. Had she overslept? A sudden disappointment at the thought of missing breakfast eased when she looked at the time. By East Coast standards, she'd slept until 10 o'clock. But in New Mexico's time zone, she was right on schedule for the morning meal.

Dressing quickly, she grabbed both her car and room keys, out of habit, before hesitating. There was no reason to drive to the café for breakfast. It was easily within walking distance and the exercise would do her good. She set her car keys back on the desk, picked up a journal, and walked to the café.

The woman who greeted her looked remarkably like Marisol, except with two additional decades under her belt. Paige knew immediately it was the young woman's mother.

"You must be Luz. I met your daughter last night," Paige said, reaching to shake the woman's hand. Instead, she received an enthusiastic embrace.

"Yes, I was so glad when Marisol told me you had arrived safely," Luz said. "I'm sorry I wasn't here to greet you. I run the resort and also a shop in Tres Palomas."

"Marisol told me about your shop. I'd love to see it when I go into town." Paige followed Luz into the café, a modest room off the main lobby.

"I would love for you to come by. Lena opens the shop for me in the mornings so that I can feed guests here, but I'll be there this afternoon. For now: some food. We have good weather today, and you will want to explore the area. You need energy. And I know you had only tamales for dinner last night."

"Which were delicious, I have to tell you," Paige said, sitting at a small table with a place setting for one. A turquoise vase held a cluster of bright red and yellow wildflowers. "It was so kind of Marisol to share them with me."

"We don't let guests go hungry." Luz smiled, then went into the kitchen. She returned moments later and placed a plate of pancakes in front of Paige, setting down a petite syrup pitcher alongside.

"These are blue corn pancakes," Luz said. "And prickly pear syrup. I'm guessing you don't eat this combination in New York."

"You're right," Paige laughed. "But I never met a pancake I didn't like. Or syrup, for that matter. And the side dish of fresh berries is perfect. It all looks delicious." She picked up a fork and cut into the pancakes, taking a bite. "And it *is* delicious." She wasted no time diving in for another bite.

"Thank you," Luz said. "I love to cook, so I'm always happy to have guests here to feed."

A phone call sent Luz scurrying to the front office, leaving Paige alone with both her pancakes and thoughts. She pushed the plate of food slightly aside and flipped open her journal to take notes. She'd already been shown such kindness since her arrival. If this was typical New Mexico hospitality, she was thanking her lucky stars that she had added personal time onto the trip. Between the people, the food and the sheer luxury of staying at a mineral springs resort, she had a perfect trip combination.

"Looks like we have unexpected guests coming in on Monday," Luz said as she returned to the café. "A tour group whose accommodations fell through in Santa Fe – some sort of flooding problem in their hotel. Remind me never to say out loud again how much I love cooking!" Luz's laughter hinted that she welcomed the idea of an incoming group.

"Is that unusual, having a group come in?" Paige stuck a fork through a blueberry and into a piece of pancake, dipping into syrup on the side of her plate.

"I wouldn't say unusual," Luz answered. "But we see more couples and individuals looking to relax in the waters or just to find some peace and quiet. It's why we have the 'whisper zone' signs in many locations. We also have private soaking areas and hiking trails. Miguel can show you around the property later this morning. We have twenty acres here at Agua Encantada, so there's room for everyone to find a little solitude."

"Is Miguel your son?"

"No," Luz said with a slight frown. "I'd like to think I would have put more sense in that brain of his if I'd been his mother. He handles maintenance at the resort along with other odds and ends. He's a good employee as long as he stays out of trouble."

"A tour of the property sounds great, if he doesn't mind," Paige said quickly. "I could make some notes for the article so that I can finish it up early. I do want to relax while I'm here, to take a few days completely off from work."

"You should have brought a friend with you." Luz smiled. "It's a good place to share with someone special. Speaking of which, Miguel is quite a ladies man, just to warn you."

"Thanks for the warning, Luz," Paige laughed. "I have a phone call to make after breakfast, but I'll track him down after that and ask for a tour. I'm sure it'll be fine."

"Like I said, I'm just warning you," Luz said. "You'll find him out by the workshop, about a hundred yards behind the spa in the center of the property."

When the phone rang again, Luz headed back to the front office. Paige scarfed up the rest of the pancakes as if she hadn't eaten a plate full of tamales just the night before. New Mexico wasn't looking to be a good place to watch calories. Not if everything she tried tasted as good as these first two meals.

As Paige stepped into the lobby, she saw that Luz was still on the phone, so she waved a silent "thank you" in her direction and walked back to her casita. Once inside, she collapsed on the bed and looked at her cell phone, happy she had service again, as well as voice mail from the previous night. It only took a couple rings after dialing before Jake picked up.

"Well, if it isn't the independent reporter, checking in," Jake laughed. "I take it you made it to New Mexico. I was getting worried – only a little, mind you. I know you can take care of yourself. But I did try calling you last night."

Paige smiled at the thought of Jake trying to reach her. She shouldn't have been happy that he was worried, yet that thought was a little bit satisfying.

"The cell service went out during a storm last night," Paige said. "I did try to call. Or at least I tried to try, until I realized there was no reception."

"Same thing happens here in storms sometimes, too," Jake said. "Anyway, how was your trip out there? You flew into Albuquerque, right?"

"Yep, and the trip was fine. Though I barely beat the storm by the time I drove up to Agua Encantada. The girl who works the reception desk brought me a plate of tamales so I wouldn't have to drive into town for dinner."

The sound of papers shuffling came through the phone. Typical, Paige thought. Jake was working on the plans, supply orders and invoices for improvements on his ranch in Jackson Hole.

"So, what's this place like?"

"It's great," Paige started off, not sure how to describe what she'd seen so far. "I'll have a better feel for it later – so far it's just initial impressions. A resort staff member is going to give me a tour of the property today. I've met the woman who manages it, Luz, as well as her daughter, Marisol. They seem nice, plus the food is great. Different from anywhere else I've traveled. Those tamales last night were delicious. And the pancakes this morning were made from blue cornmeal and served with prickly pear syrup. The food itself tells me the area is unique. I'm eager to explore."

"You do fall into assignments with exceptional culinary benefits," Jake teased, "though it would be hard to find anything like the dishes Mist cooked up in Timberton when you were hunting down sapphires for your last article. You do know that you don't write a food column, right? Maybe you should. You could take me along as an official taste tester."

So far, Paige and Jake had only seen each other when her assignments happened to be within driving distance of Jake's Jackson Hole ranch. An image of traveling with Jake ran through Paige's mind, and the idea that he might come out on an assignment with her was appealing, though this would certainly bring up questions about where they were headed romantically. She tried not to think about the nature of their relationship because of the limits imposed by distance. She saw no point in being frustrated or in getting her hopes up about the future.

"Paige, are you listening? I asked what your plan is for your first day, today."

"Of course I'm listening to you," Paige lied. *How ironic that I'm not listening to you because I'm thinking about you....* "I'm going to tour the property and then drive into town. I want to see Luz's shop, plus get an overview of the area."

"Try not to get in trouble this time, OK?"

"Who, me? In trouble?" Paige laughed. Her reputation was well established. Curiosity was often her biggest downfall. She decided it was best not to mention her escapade outside the spa building the night before. "OK, I'll try."

"Promise me, Paige. You're there to relax, as well as to work, this time. I worry about you. It was obvious Jake was fighting to keep his tone light.

"Yes, I promise." Paige sighed. She couldn't blame him for worrying. He'd helped her out of risky situations before. Being fiercely independent, she'd prefer not to have anyone forced to come to her rescue, anyway, whether he was a handsome cowboy or not.

"I'll check in with you later," Jake said.

"That would be nice," Paige said. "More than nice, even." She was certain she could hear Jake smiling on the other end of the line. After reassuring him she'd stay out of trouble, she ended the call and headed out to tour the resort.

CHAPTER FOUR

The tall figure leaned against a tree, both thumbs shoved in the front pockets of his jeans, one foot kicked across the other. He hunched forward slightly, a result of pressing the small of his back against the tree. A thick braid of hair fell forward over his left shoulder, its color alternating black to brown as wind cast swaying shadows of leaves from above. Torn denim revealed coffee-colored thighs, a close match to the slightly darker forearms extending from rolled up shirtsleeves. He lifted the fingers of one hand in greeting as Paige approached, his thumb never leaving the pocket, his back never leaving the tree. A smile crept across his face as his eyes took in Paige.

Not subtle, Paige thought, watching the man's eyes travel down the length of her body and back up to meet her eyes. A brief flutter ran up her spine. Nothing on the man's face gave any clue to the thoughts hidden behind the dark brown eyes that stared back at her. She stopped a good eight feet away and, without meaning to, frowned.

"*Sonrisa*." The low, smooth voiced startled Paige, who tried, unsuccessfully, to come up with a response to the unfamiliar greeting.

"I will call you *Sonrisa*," he repeated. "It means 'smile.' Something you should think about doing. It would suit your pretty face, *amiga*."

"My name is Paige."

"Yes, I know that already. Luz has told me about you." The man pushed forward, away from the tree. He took several steps directly toward Paige before veering away to circle her. "You are here to write about our waters."

"That's right," Paige said, spinning slowly to keep him in sight. "And you are Miguel. Luz said you could show me around the property. If you don't mind, that is."

"Yes, I am Miguel," he said, looking out across the grounds, as if surveying the area he was about to show her. Without looking back at Paige, he added, "She did not tell me you were so beautiful."

Paige shifted her weight and crossed her arms, annoyed.

"The property?" Paige repeated.

"I would be delighted to show it to you, *Sonrisa*," Miguel said. "Right this way." He turned abruptly, leaving Paige to follow.

"As you know, the guest casitas are over there." Miguel waved his arm toward Paige's little house. In addition to several cottages that sat on either side of hers, two more rows of lodging ran behind her building. Some units were attached to others, while some stood alone. All had a porch or patio by the front door with one or two chairs for sitting.

"How many casitas altogether?" Paige asked, taking in the layout of the various buildings.

"Seventeen," Miguel said. "Some are larger than others."

"Do many families visit?"

"Some, but most of the guests are here alone or in couples. We allow children, but the facilities are limited. The pool hours are restricted to adults during mornings and evenings. Young children do not have many options here. Older kids enjoy it if they like reading or other quiet activities."

"That leaves out a lot of kids these days. Unless they can play video games or hang out online," Paige said.

"Exactly," Miguel said. "We do have wifi here, but this is not the right environment for them if that is what they are looking for."

"I can see that," Paige said, following Miguel as he switched directions and walked away from the lodgings.

"This is our spa area." Miguel indicated the adobe building and a gated area that Paige already knew too well. Landscaped by nature, boulders and cacti surrounded outdoor pools. Rustic lounge chairs offered resting areas or tanning spots for those wishing to soak up the sun. "Our waters are very famous. People come from far away to enjoy their healing properties. Iron, arsenic and soda all offer different benefits. My sister will explain more about that when you meet her."

"Your sister?"

"Yes, Ana, my younger sister, works in the spa part time and spends the rest of her time making jewelry. She is a wonderful artist. You will see some of her pieces in the gift store."

"Oh, I saw some of her work when I checked in. It's fabulous. You must be proud of her, your parents, too."

"Yes, I am. She is my heart, my only family. We lost our parents to a bad accident when we were in our teens. I was nineteen; she was only thirteen. You could say that I raised her, though it may be the other way around. I want her to succeed. I would do anything to help her."

Turning, Miguel pointed to a set of rustic buildings set apart from the main spa area. Paige saw four circular adobe walls, spaced a good thirty feet apart. A pathway led toward them, breaking into four individual paths about halfway to the structures.

"Are those private accommodations?"

"Private, yes, but accommodations, no," Miguel said. "Those are individual mineral pools that guests can reserve. Each has walls for privacy, but no roof, so guests can soak in the pools and see the sky during the daytime or the stars at night. There is a kiva fireplace in each one, too."

"It sounds wonderful," Paige sighed. "Romantic for couples who come to visit."

"Yes, the private soaking pools are very popular. Along with towels, we offer beverages for guests using those – chilled water and tea, I think. Ana will be able to tell you exactly."

"So there are no roofs? What about rain?"

Miguel laughed. "Many guests soak, even in the rain. And, if we need to, we can roll out a tarp across the top of the building. Each private complex has one, rigged up to a pulley."

Paige hesitated and then followed as Miguel changed directions again and headed down a trail that led away from the resort. All she could see from where they stood was a barn with surrounding fencing and an old pick-up truck parked nearby. She glanced back, torn between playing it safe by returning to her room and trying not to insult Miguel by behaving as if she didn't trust him completely. In the end, she stuck with the tour and continued down the trail until they arrived at the barn.

"I want you to meet some friends of mine," Miguel said, a hint of mischief in his tone. "Especially Josie, one of the hottest chicks I have ever known."

Now that's just plain rude, Paige thought as she watched Miguel disappear around the corner of the barn. Didn't this man have any class? Couldn't he see that the respect he clearly had for his sister should extend to other women, as well? Paige was still bristling when Miguel reappeared, one arm trailing behind, holding a thick rope. In a few seconds, a tall leggy creature with baby doll eyes and soft, curly hair appeared.

"Paige, meet Josie," Miguel said. He broke into a wide grin as Paige took in the elegant llama on the end of the rope.

"Well, aren't you just the funny guy, Miguel." Paige stood back as she and Josie sized each other up.

"I do my best, *Sonrisa*. Now come say hello. Josie does not bite."

"But she might spit, or so I've always thought."

Miguel shook his head. "That is a misconception. All animals have behaviors they can exhibit when they feel threatened or nervous. It does not mean they always will. Josie is comfortable now. She trusts me, so she trusts you."

Paige sighed. "You're giving that llama credit for a lot of reasoning, you know."

"Well, she is a smart one," Miguel answered, patting Josie on the head and running his hand down the back of her long neck. "Now, Rico is another story. He is just your everyday goofball."

"I'm afraid to ask, but who's Rico?"

Another llama, this one darker, with sleepy eyes and an awkward, comical gait, emerged from the barn and peered over the fence. Paige could swear he looked her up and down the same way Miguel had earlier. Miguel read her thoughts and laughed, slapping Rico playfully on the back. "That is my boy. You see how he likes you?"

Paige tilted her head sideways and took a good look at Rico. "What I see is a smirk on his face that is starting to look mighty familiar. Do llamas pick up expressions from their caretakers?"

"Now, now, *Sonrisa*. I have given you this perfect tour and you choose to insult me," Miguel said. Only the gleam in his eyes told Paige he was kidding.

"You're right," she admitted. "You've given me an excellent introduction to Agua Encantada. And I appreciate it. I should get back now and jot some notes down, if you won't mind me leaving you here."

"That is fine. I need to fill Josie and Rico's water trough and set up their food for the day. Anything else you need, you just come find me." Leading Josie with the rope, Miguel took her back into the barn, returning quickly for Rico when he refused to follow.

"I am telling you, *Sonrisa*, Rico is quite taken with you."

"Really, I don't think so," Paige countered.

"I do not think so, either. I know so." Miguel gave Rico a light swat and sent him back into the barn. He waved to Paige and disappeared into the barn, as well.

Paige turned back toward the resort, retracing her way up the trail. So far Agua Encantada was proving to be full of surprises. And she had a feeling more were in store.

CHAPTER FIVE

Paige picked up one of the small pottery pieces, inspecting it more closely. Though displayed between larger items and only a few inches high, the figure of a woman had caught her attention. The black lines and burnt red blended into the natural coloring of the clay. Something about the petite figurine was both solid and delicate. It was just one of many fascinating pieces that made Paige glad she'd chosen Luz's store as her first in-town destination.

"Tell me about this piece, Luz," Paige said, turning toward the shopkeeper.

"Intriguing, isn't it?" Luz stepped around the counter and moved closer to Paige. "This is a storyteller doll. Note the open mouth and the small children seated on and around the central figure."

"A storyteller," Paige echoed. "Yes, I can see it. A traditional piece of pottery, I suppose?"

"Well, yes and no," Luz replied. "Traditional in the sense that oral history has always played an important role in Native American culture. This is how stories have been passed down from generation to generation. But storyteller dolls don't go back far. The first was made by Helen Cordero in 1964."

"That recently?" Paige raised her eyebrows and set the small figure back on the shelf.

"Yes," Luz said. "Helen Cordero was an artist from the Cochiti pueblo, not far from here. She spent many years doing beadwork and leatherwork with her husband's cousin, Juanita Arquero, but switched to pottery in the 1950s. When the bowls she made turned out crooked, she became discouraged until her cousin suggested she switch to figures. She has been quoted as saying that the process of making the figures was '…like a flower blooming.' They were an immediate success. Folk art collector Alexander Girard of Santa Fe bought all of her small figurines and asked her to make more. Inspired by memories of her grandfather, Santiago Quintana, telling stories to his grandchildren, she made the first storyteller doll, a male figure with five small listeners gathered around."

Paige leaned forward and looked at the figure again. "They are all children, the smaller figures, aren't they?"

"True," Luz replied. "But Helen Cordero didn't call them children. She called them 'little listeners.' She felt stories were passed on because they were heard, not because they were told."

"Is she still alive?" Paige asked.

"No," Luz smiled. "She was born in 1915 and died in 1994. She didn't start making the storyteller dolls until her children were grown. But many artists are making the dolls these days, hundreds."

"They're amazing, these figures."

"You might want to hear some actual storytelling while you're here, too." Luz tilted her head to the side and paused before continuing. "The tradition has continued from generation to generation. An old woman in this town gathers people around her every week to tell tales passed down from her own elders."

"Right here in Tres Palomas?"

"Yes." Luz nodded. "Every Sunday after *la Misa*, she waits, sitting on the edge of the tile fountain in the church courtyard. She doesn't speak until a small crowd has gathered and settled around her."

"Like a storyteller doll."

"Yes, like that." Luz paused, a slight frown crossing her face. "She's always very quiet, very serious, while talking. Most of the stories are legends that we've all heard since we were 'little listeners' ourselves. A few stories are not familiar, though. I don't know where she gets them."

"She could be making them up," Paige suggested.

"Maybe," Luz said. "She loves the children who come to hear her, so I'm sure she uses her imagination. But some stories seem to upset her. She gets emotional and raises her voice. Once I saw her stare above the heads of the children, gather her shawl around her and leave without a word of goodbye. Many of her stories are about animals, which is common for legends. But she will never tell a story about a snake. She lost a son to a snakebite many years ago. It was terrible. But the rattlers out here are dangerous, especially the babies."

"How awful," Paige exclaimed. "Does she have other family alive?"

"Only one much younger brother," Luz said. "She lives alone, in a small room behind the church. Cleans and helps with chores in exchange for a place to live. Her stories entertain others, but they aren't enough to lighten the sadness inside her."

"What is her name?"

"People just call her *Abuela*. Grandmother." Luz said. "We all love her; the whole town does. Most of us grew up listening to her stories every week."

The bells on the door jangled, and a young woman entered. Luz excused herself to greet the new customer. Paige turned back toward the display case, looking at the clay figurines again and then moving on to admire a flat, glass case of jewelry. Necklaces and rings, bracelets and earrings caught the glow of a bright display light above. Turquoise and coral added life to sleek silver settings. One slender chain caught her attention, a pendant in the shape of a rabbit dangling from the end. She leaned forward, twisting her head sideways in an attempt to see the price tag buried halfway under a wire stand that displayed the piece. Luz reappeared at her side.

"*Muy hermoso*," Luz said. "A beautiful piece. These necklaces are good sellers. Not as expensive as the bulky pieces, more affordable for visitors. Still, they bring in a good price, since they are handcrafted. You can take the necklace out of the case. The top of the display lifts up. A local artist named Ana makes them. I'm sure you'll meet her since she manages the spa at our resort."

"Ah, yes, Miguel's sister. He mentioned her when he showed me around the property earlier." Paige reached inside the case and carefully lifted the necklace off the stand, checking the price tag at the same time. It was expensive, fifty dollars, but reasonable for the quality. Raising it up, she watched the light hit the silver rabbit as it moved freely below the chain. Tiny inlaid stones of turquoise, coral and malachite enhanced the already beautiful design. "Does she make many different designs?"

"Not too many," Luz replied. "Her pieces are usually rabbits, turtles and horses. She also has a beautiful design with three doves that is very unique, both in a pin and in earrings, like you see in the case. She only makes a few of those. That design represents our village, Tres Palomas."

Luz reached out for the necklace, offering to replace it in the display, but Paige shook her head. "I'd like to buy this. I don't have anything like it, and I love to support local artists when I travel. In fact, I'll take the earrings with the silver doves, too."

"Wonderful choices," Luz said as she moved behind the cash register. She pulled tissue paper from below the counter, wrapping the jewelry in it before ringing up the purchase. "You travel a lot, don't you? For your job?"

Paige nodded as she handed over a credit card. "I have been this past year. We've been running a series on the Old West, so every couple of months I head somewhere new. The last two assignments were farther north, in Wyoming and Montana."

"Ah, cowboy country," Luz smiled.

"Yes," Paige laughed. "Cowboy country, indeed." A soft blush crept up her neck, something Luz caught.

"I sense a non-work related story here," Luz prodded lightly. "Something to be continued, maybe?" She slipped the necklace and earrings into a small brown bag.

Paige sighed as she signed the credit card receipt and handed it back. Her phone call with Jake earlier emphasized just how far away she was from him this time with slim chance of seeing him. The distance between Wyoming and New Mexico was just too great.

"Maybe," Paige said, more to avoid an answer than anything else. It was a question she asked herself often. As much as she yearned to see Jake, the long-distance relationship was proving hard. With two thousand miles between them most of the time and nearly one thousand on this particular assignment, meeting up was a long shot at best.

"Thank you, Luz," Paige added quickly, taking the bag from the shopkeeper. "I'd better get back. What time is dinner again?"

"Anytime between 6 and 8 o'clock," Luz said. "We may have more guests checking in later today. No reservations, but we've had some phone calls. So you may have company. And Miguel will be there, since he knows I'm fixing *Pollo con Mole*. He never misses that."

"*Pollo con Mole*?" Paige repeated, attempting the correct pronunciation.

Luz laughed. "Chicken with a delicious sauce of tomatoes, chiles and chocolate. *Delicioso*. You'll see."

"Sounds perfect, Luz," Paige laughed. "Anything with chocolate in it gets my stamp of approval. I'll see you at dinner."

Paige left the store and drove through town, slowing down to gather initial impressions. Most of the architecture was short and squat, some wood, but most adobe, painted in earthy tan and pale peach. They blended in with the dusty streets seamlessly. A few structures boasted door or window frames in brilliant turquoise or red, setting them apart from the other, generally drab buildings. One house featured window boxes with bright flowers, but more stood behind gardens of cactus and sage.

Two barefoot children ran out into the street after a ball, causing Paige to brake quickly. Not looking, they laughed, gathered the ball and ran back to an unfenced front yard that was littered with play equipment – a tricycle on its side, a metal swing set with one working, and one broken, seat. In the yard next door, shirts, pants and dresses dangled from a clothesline. A plump woman pulled a pair of denim jeans off the line, dropping them into a plastic basket on the ground below.

The harsh reality of daily life in Tres Palomas was apparent to Paige. Only a few miles from the resort, luxury played no part in the average lifestyle of the town's residents. The focus was on survival, on feeding children, on keeping a roof over each family's heads.

The peel of bells drew Paige's attention to the opposite side of the road, where a side street headed off at an angle, dead-ending a block later in front of a church. The whitewashed adobe structure sat behind a walled courtyard, its rounded silhouette topped off with a bell tower. A tile fountain like the one Luz had described filled the center of the courtyard.

Paige turned the car into the side street and pulled up in front of the church. A rustic sign announced times for Mass on Sunday. *La Misa*, as Luz had phrased it. So this was where the old woman they called Abuela told her stories. The courtyard was deserted now, but she could imagine crowds surrounding the woman on Sundays. It was something she wanted to see and hear for herself. She would make a point of it.

CHAPTER SIX

Miguel pulled the old Ford into an empty space in front of the Coyote Cantina. He set the parking brake, twisted his keys in the ignition, and listened to the engine die. As he stepped out of the truck, dust and gravel flew up around his feet. He glanced at the deserted lot. Charlie Whitehorse should've been there by then. It was a rare day that the old guy wasn't into his fourth beer by late afternoon. For that matter, a few locals often closed up their businesses for the afternoon to settle in for coffee and jalapeño poppers, a combination of flavors that Miguel could never understand.

He elbowed the truck door and let its own weight swing it shut, oddly annoyed by the sound of metal against metal as it closed. He was rattled, though he couldn't pinpoint a reason. Nothing looked out of the ordinary, aside from the excess of empty parking spaces. But, call it instinct: call it premonition – something didn't feel right.

As with any other afternoon, Juanita stood behind the bar, leaning forward against the counter, alternating her attention between the door and a local paper. Her wrinkled, weathered skin gave away every one of her seventy-something years. Her toughness revealed decades of harsh living.

"Where is everyone, Juanita?" Miguel took a seat at the bar.

"How the hell should I know?" Juanita grabbed a Corona from a low refrigerator and popped off the cap. She slid it in front of Miguel and smacked her hand against the countertop. "Four bucks, youngster, cough it up."

"C'mon, Juanita, you know everything that goes on in these parts. How long have you been running this place? Ten, fifteen years?" Miguel winked at her before lifting the bottle to his lips and taking a long draw. He set the bottle back on the bar and exhaled, then repeated the action. Reaching into his shirt pocket, he pulled out a stack of crumpled bills and tossed them on the counter.

The old bartender laughed, her voice scratchy and sharp. "Twenty-seven years and not one day short of that. And maybe most days I do know what's going on around here, but not today, *amigo*. Today I'm minding my own business." She pulled four single dollar bills from the tangled cluster of money, flattened them and stuck them in the cash register.

"It does not look like you have much business to mind," Miguel said. "Not unless you are hiding customers in the back room."

"It's not the busiest day I've had. Not sure what this town's coming to when it's four in the afternoon and no one's drinking yet." Juanita rinsed out a bar rag and wiped down the counter. Tossing the rag aside, she ran her hands along her jeans to dry them. "What kind of trouble are you into today?"

"My hands are clean," Miguel said, releasing the beer bottle long enough to raise both hands in the air.

Juanita shook her head. "I don't believe everything I see." She grabbed a bucket from below the counter and headed to the back, her voice trailing behind her. "Your hands might look squeaky clean when you wave them around like that, but there's not a day I've known you that you weren't in trouble or at least looking for it."

Miguel watched her leave the room, listened to the sound of ice being shoveled into the bucket. She was right, of course. He often managed to fall on the wrong side of the law, or at least the wrong side of common sense. And he was pretty sure what he was wrapped up in now was taking him down one of those paths.

He took another slug of beer, then swiveled around on the stool to look out the window. The lot was as deserted as it had been when he walked in. He tilted the bottle up again, finishing the beer.

"I was hoping to find Whitehorse here. He owes me money"

"You and everybody else."

The sound of ice filling a bucket continued, drowning out Juanita's comments, but Miguel didn't need to hear them to know what she was saying. Charlie Whitehorse owed just about everyone in the town money, except for those who were smart enough to not fall for his sob stories.

As if on cue, Charlie Whitehorse walked in, taking his usual spot at the end of the bar. He was a creature of habit when it came to that sort of thing. Just as he was about other aspects of his life – like not paying money back on time.

Juanita emerged from the back with a full bucket of ice. She emptied it into a bin behind the bar and pulled out a bottle of beer, setting it in front of Whitehorse.

Miguel slid over onto the next bar stool and motioned to Juanita for another beer. She tipped a glass at an angle and filled it with draft. Setting it down in front of Miguel, she caught his eye and raised her eyebrows, then moved away. She'd heard plenty of discussions between Whitehorse and

Miguel. Their voices always went up a few notches during disagreements.

"I came by earlier looking for you, Whitehorse. It is not like you to wait until evening to hit Juanita up for a beer."

"So? I don't live my life by your time schedule, Miguel. Besides, why not just stick around, then? You know I'll end up here at some point."

"And miss Luz's *Pollo con Mole*? Even tracking you down is not worth that."

"For once we agree." Whitehorse let out a grunt that halfway resembled a laugh.

"Listen, you need to get me that money," Miguel said, lowering his voice. He lifted the beer to his mouth and chugged half of it without pausing. Setting the glass down, he cleared his throat. "You said there would not be any more delays."

The older man mumbled something into his drink.

"What did you say?" Miguel swirled the beer around in his glass, staring down into the foamy liquid.

"I said your sister should be grateful for the sales," Whitehorse said. "Tell her to be patient. You know how rich people can be – taking their time paying things because they have no idea what it's like to wait for money. Ana should just be thankful I found her some customers. This town isn't exactly a tourist destination, aside from the spa. She can only sell so much around here." He slid the empty beer bottle in Juanita's direction and motioned for another. Juanita brought one over, along with another draft for Miguel, and returned to the other end of the bar.

Miguel said nothing, set his empty glass aside. Whitehorse cast a curious glance at him and then raised his eyebrows. "Wait...don't tell me. You took them without telling her?"

Miguel remained quiet.

Whitehorse slapped his hand down on the counter and laughed. "Well, there you go. You steal your own sister's jewelry and then blame me for not paying for it."

"That is not what happened and you know it!" Miguel caught his voice rising and lowered it quickly. "I would never steal from her. You said you had buyers for some of her pieces and I wanted to get her the money before telling her, as a surprise. You needed to deliver the jewelry in order to get the money. The whole thing should have taken a couple days at most."

"You can't tell me you weren't planning on skimming a bit off the top of those sales yourself. Stop trying to act like you're only doing your sister a favor. I still remember you stealing oranges from Madre's Mercado and selling them on the highway, telling people they were from your own backyard. We don't even grow oranges here."

"I was fourteen, Whitehorse. And this is about business, not favors. What I do with the money for selling the pieces does not concern you. I will give Ana what she always gets for her work."

"You're blowing this out of proportion, *amigo*. We're only talking about eight pieces of jewelry. By the way, did you manage to get more? I can get you a payment faster if we rack up their bill." Whitehorse nodded his head, pleased with himself for thinking of this angle.

"You can forget about getting your hands on any other pieces. You already have one each of Ana's best designs, and I never should have gotten you those. It takes her time to make each piece. And she needs to buy new supplies as they sell. She deserves to be paid right away."

"Maybe you should've thought of all that when you gave them to me to begin with," Whitehorse said. He stood up, finished his beer. "I'm doing you and your sister a favor by selling her jewelry. You don't have the same connections I have. Without me, your sister would just be selling one piece here and one piece there instead of eight pieces at once. Relax. I'll have your money to you by the end of the week."

"See that you do," Miguel said, watching Whitehorse saunter out of the cantina.

Miguel kept his eyes on the retreating figure.

Behind him, Juanita said, "You should know better than to try to do business with Charlie Whitehorse, Miguel."

"And you should know better than to tell me that, Juanita."

Juanita ignored the last remark as she wiped the bar countertop down with a rag. "I still hold out hope for you, Miguel. One of these days you'll wake up and decide to walk a straight line."

Miguel smiled. He stood up and tossed a handful of crumpled dollar bills on the counter.

"Just try to stay out of trouble for a change," Juanita cautioned.

"Do not hold your breath," Miguel laughed.

"Trust me," Juanita said. "I won't."

CHAPTER SEVEN

When Paige stepped inside the spa, the cool scent of eucalyptus and flowing tones of panpipes wrapped around her like morning mist. She blinked, her eyes adjusting to the soft interior lighting after the bright sun. Within seconds, her stress began to ease. This was what she'd anticipated since first hearing about the assignment. As much as she loved her work, she was long overdue for some personal time.

"Are you here for a treatment?" the receptionist asked. She smiled at Paige before looking down at an appointment book. Her dark hair flowed loose around her shoulders, one side pinned back behind her ear with a yellow raffia flower. A silver and turquoise necklace sat above the gathered neckline of her white blouse. Paige recognized the design as a simple variation of a squash-blossom pattern.

"A massage or facial? Or maybe a lavender herbal wrap or salt glow scrub?"

"No, though that all sounds tempting," Paige admitted. "Maybe another day, but I'm just here to soak in the mineral waters. I understand the pools are known for their different health benefits."

"Yes, they are," the young woman said as she pulled a bundle with a robe and gel slippers from a shelf behind the desk along with a locker key and handed them to Paige. "We have three different types of pools here that you can soak in: iron, soda and arsenic. The iron pool helps your immune system and blood flow. The arsenic and soda pools will help relieve stiffness in your joints. They are also good for your digestive system and skin. I suggest trying them all."

"I imagine you get this question a lot, but isn't arsenic poisonous? How is that pool safe?" Paige said.

A light smile crossed the receptionist's face. Yes, the question had been asked many times.

"There are only trace amounts in the water. Arsenic is only dangerous at certain levels. Smaller amounts have healing qualities."

"I see." Attempting a non-skeptical attitude, Paige leaned forward to read the young woman's nametag.

"You're Ana, Miguel's sister," she said. "You're the one who makes the jewelry."

"Yes."

"Your designs are beautiful," Paige said. "I bought a necklace at Luz's shop, as well as the earrings with the three birds. I've never seen anything quite like them before, so beautiful."

"Thank you. Those are the doves of our town, Tres Palomas," Ana said, smiling. "It is a favorite design of mine."

Paige wrapped her arms around the bathrobe and slippers and headed for the dressing room, which Ana pointed out with a soft sway of her arm. The hallway through the spa building was narrow and cool, with sparse artwork along the walls. The minimalism gave Paige the feeling of leaving the sensory overload of the outside world behind. She'd entered a new, soothing territory.

A row of lockers lined one wall in the changing area, and wooden benches ran the middle length of the room. Paige set her belongings on a bench and opened a nearby locker. She took her time removing her outer clothing and hanging it neatly on hooks. Leaving on her swimsuit, she pulled the soft bathrobe around her and slipped her feet into the gel slippers. She gathered her hair and twisted it up into a clip, leaving her neck and shoulders free.

The spa ambiance encouraged reverence. Paige found herself paying attention to details she normally wouldn't have noticed: the cool sensation of her bare feet sliding into the molded form of the slippers, the click of the locker door as she closed it. Each sound and movement felt deliberate.

Paige left the dressing room and continued down the hall until she reached the entrance to the back courtyard. Stepping outside, she paused momentarily in the brighter light to adjust her senses once again. A peace surpassed the energy of the direct sunlight. Sculpted works dotted the outdoor space, separated by stone pathways and desert gardens. A labyrinth filled the center of the courtyard, its entrance beckoning guests to walk the circular paths.

The iron pool rested against a solid rock wall, surrounded by smaller rock formations. Paige slipped off the robe and draped it over a ceramic bench, removing the slippers and sliding them underneath. Dipping one toe over the side of the pool, she pulled back as the water's heat registered. What had the brochure said? The temperature was something like 104 degrees? She would need to ease her way in.

Sitting on the edge of the pool, Paige slipped one foot in, then the other, lowering her legs slowly as her skin adjusted to the hot water. Once the temperature became tolerable, she eased the rest of her body in, catching her breath several times as waves of heat encircled new sections of skin. Finally, the warmth of the pool reached her neck. She leaned back against the edge of the pool and closed her eyes.

The mood of Agua Encantada inspired a wider contemplation of the world than Manhattan did. Between the warmth of the mineral water against her skin, the hot mist around her face and the lack of distracting noise, her mind ventured off on a trip of its own. As Paige gave into the calming effect of the water, she opened her eyes and took in the spa grounds – the blue salvia swaying in the wind, the terra cotta tones of the buildings and the blooming cactus that lined the edge of the property. She let go of schedules, assignments and itineraries and relaxed into the moment. She felt liberated.

Her job as a reporter didn't allow for much flexibility, though when she traveled, she got a respite from some of the daily deadlines and demands. Most trips were just long enough for her to want more time. Although she'd managed to extend assignments once or twice, she'd planned the visit to Agua Encantada specifically to allow her to do more than work. The assignment was simple, a quick write-up about the mineral springs and their history. It left room for personal time.

A flush of heat crept across Paige's face, reminding her she'd been soaking for a while. She opened her eyes and brought her legs in underneath her, standing up to allow cool air to pass across her upper torso. Lifting herself out of the water with her arms, she swung her legs around onto the edge of the pool. As she leaned back against the concrete, a light wind passed through the courtyard. The mixture of solitude, warm skin and soft breeze felt luxurious. When had she been this relaxed? She couldn't remember.

"Lookin' good, *Sonrisa*."

Paige tensed. She turned her head to find Miguel a few feet away, both his hands and chin balanced on the end of a broom. She cupped one hand over her eyes.

"You shouldn't sneak up on people like that, Miguel," Paige said, quickly fighting her annoyance at the disruption. She wasn't about to let him chase away the benefit of her relaxing soak.

"I did not mean to," Miguel said. "I usually sweep the area this time of day. I did not expect anyone to be here."

"Well, here I am." Paige sighed, easing her head back down on the pavement and dropping her arm back by her side. "Go right ahead. Sweep away. Sweep around me. Sweep anywhere you'd like. Just don't make me move. I think that water melted my bones."

Miguel laughed. "Yes, it does that. It is one of the reasons people have been coming here for centuries – first the Tewa Indians, then the Spaniards and now reporters from New York."

Paige smiled in spite of herself. Even though annoying, Miguel had a sense of humor.

"We have lounge chairs back against the spa building," he said as he started to sweep. "You do not have to lie on the concrete."

"I know, I saw them," Paige replied. "But it was all I could do to pull myself out of the pool. I doubt my muscles have the strength to move over there. Besides, the pavement feels warm. I never would have thought of concrete as soothing, but it is."

"The sun shares its warmth with the ground, which then shares it with you. Wait until you try the mud bath treatment here."

"I'm not so sure that's going to happen," Paige laughed. "I understand soaking in hot water, but mud?"

"It is good for the skin, city girl. You should read the brochures." Miguel moved to another section of the spa courtyard and resumed sweeping. "Cleans your pores or something like that."

"Something like that?" Paige repeated. "That's a weak sales pitch if I ever heard one. Have you tried the mud bath yourself?"

"No time. Always something that needs tending to around here. If not around the casitas and spa, then out by the llama barn and storage buildings."

A radio clipped to Miguel's belt crackled.

"There, you see? That will be Marisol," Miguel said. "Which means I will leave you in peace. Do not fall asleep on that pavement. It will get cooler as the afternoon moves on."

Paige listened to Miguel's footsteps as he disappeared inside the spa building. She drew her knees up, placed the soles of her feet flat on the ground and pressed the small of her back into the warm concrete. Leaves skittered across the pool area as the wind picked up, scratching the ground lightly. She inhaled deeply, exhaling at a slow, steady rhythm. It was a rare, perfect moment, the kind that crept up without warning and washed over a person like a sudden breeze.

Getting to know other people had not been part of her plan for this trip. She did that often enough on assignments. This time she had intended to observe from a distance, picking up information from personal exploration and adding to it from printed information in brochures and online. But she could already feel herself getting pulled into the stories of Tres Palomas' residents – the jewelry artist, the woman who told stories in the church courtyard, and the mother/daughter team of Luz and Marisol. Maybe it wasn't the different locations she visited that intrigued her. Maybe it was the people and their individual stories. And secrets…there were always secrets behind the façades of the places she visited.

Sitting up, Paige lowered her legs into the pool again, but remained seated on the edge. She dropped her head forward and let the breeze sweep across her shoulders and neck. Had she ever taken time like this to be alone on assignments? To just sit, surrounded only by her thoughts, the wind and the absence of pressure? She thought about her life in New York, travel memories, plans for the future. So much was undefined in her life. This allowed her freedom, which she'd always craved. But somewhere inside her she heard a soft voice suggesting there was something more. She'd been hearing the same light voice ever since she met Jake Norris for the first time, in Jackson Hole.

Paige pulled her legs out of the water and stood, moving across the courtyard to the row of lounge chairs that Miguel had mentioned. She spread her towel across one and stretched out. Without thinking, she reached to one side of the chair with her arm, and then the other. What was she looking for, anyway? Her cell phone? A book? Something, anything to occupy her mind, rather than simply relaxing? How strange it felt just to let the time pass. How odd that something so simple should be so challenging.

Paige allowed the warm sun and light breeze to take over as she willed her unquiet mind to let go. She cleared her thoughts and, relaxing into the chair, drifted off to sleep.

CHAPTER EIGHT

Two stately church doors were propped open when Paige pulled up in front of St. Bernadette's. The parish priest stood on the top step, shaking the hands of departing parishioners – young girls in flowered dresses and pigtails, teenage boys who shuffled obediently alongside parents, and elderly church members who leaned on walkers. A few cars were already pulling out of parking spaces, while others posed with open doors as passengers climbed in.

In the courtyard, a half-dozen people waited patiently while an older woman stepped up to the center fountain and took a seat. She eased herself back until her legs dangled off the ground, looking like a young girl trapped in an old woman's body. As she settled, those around her also took seats, prepared to listen. Abuela's court was now in session. Paige parked her car and moved in close enough to hear.

The old woman raised a shaky hand in the air and moved it across the crowd, making eye contact with the group as her fingers pointed to each eager listener. The faces of those who surrounded her were focused, ready to absorb every word. Children, in particular, sat with wide, eager eyes.

"Today I will tell you of the Wind Bird and what happened when he broke his wing." Abuela adjusted her sitting position and rested both hands on her knees. "A man and his wife and sons lived on the seashore, where the waves grew fierce during a storm. Night and day the wind blew and the family could not fish or build a fire. They became hungry and ill and one of the sons feared for his family."

Two children resembling brother and sister shuffled onto the fountain steps. Without looking at them, Abuela paused, waiting for them to sit before continuing. The girl, who appeared to be five or six years old, pulled a rag doll into her lap. She put one finger to her lips and looked intently at the doll to hush it.

"Worried about food, the son decided to wander along the water's edge, looking for fish that may have been cast ashore during the storm, but he found none. As the wind grew fiercer, he came to a giant boulder on the Edge of the Sky and waded through the water until he reached it. On top of it, he found Wind Bird, flapping his wings. He offered to carry the bird across the water to the soft sand and Wind Bird agreed. But the water was filled with slippery rocks and the son fell, breaking one of Wind Bird's wings."

Paige glanced across the faces in the crowd. The children who had shuffled positions looked worried. Several adults wore soft smiles.

"The son fixed Wind Bird's broken wing and told him to be still," Abuela continued. "And so he was still for many days, until the waters of the sea didn't move and the fish grew sick. The son then told Wind Bird he must see if his wing was healed. Wind Bird flapped his wings and found the broken wing had healed. As the wind came back, the waves returned and the fish became well. The man and his wife and sons had food again, as did all the people who lived on the sea's edge. The Wind Bird remained friends of the people, and to this day he sometimes blows wind and sometimes leaves the sea calm."

The young girl clapped her hands, delighted with the story. "Tell us another story, Abuela. Tell us about how Rabbit lost his tail."

The old woman nodded, running her wrinkled hands along her faded skirt. Paige noticed the hem was only partially stitched, leaving a portion of the fabric hanging lower than the rest.

"Many worlds ago, Rabbit had a very long tail," Abuela said as she looked at the young girl. She paused and moved her eyes around the crowd, as if to make sure each person understood the starting point of the story. "It was a beautiful tail, even more beautiful than Fox's tail. Rabbit liked to brag about it. One winter day Fox grew tired of listening to Rabbit boast. He went down to the lake and cut a hole in the ice. He tied four fish to his tail and dropped the tail in the water."

"Wasn't his tail cold?" the young girl asked.

"You must listen to the story, *mi hija*," the old woman said.

"Yes, Fox's tail was cold, but he did not have to wait long before Rabbit came hopping along and asked Fox what he was doing. Fox told Rabbit he was fishing and pulled his tail out of the water, showing him the four fish. 'I will trade these fish for a set of beautiful tail combs in the village. There is only one set and I must have them,' Fox said. Rabbit hopped up and down and decided he must have the tail combs for himself, since he had the most beautiful tail. Fox showed Rabbit how to sit with his tail in the lake and left him there for the night."

The young girl giggled and the storyteller paused until she quieted down.

"When Fox returned in the morning, Rabbit was shaking and his teeth were chattering. 'Show me how many fish you caught,' Fox said. Rabbit tried to pull his tail out, but couldn't because it was frozen in the lake. 'Help me, Fox,' Rabbit said. So Fox smiled and gave Rabbit a big push, which sent him flying far from the ice hole. But his tail stayed stuck in the ice. And that is why Rabbit's tail is so short to this day."

The old woman stood; the story session was over.

"But tell us about the boxes, Abuela!" The young girl clapped her hands with enthusiasm. The boy sitting next to her pushed her shoulder and corrected her.

"Foxes, you silly girl," the boy next to her said. "Abuela is talking about foxes, not boxes." He rolled his eyes, clearly disgusted with the girl's confusion.

"I know the difference between foxes and boxes," the girl shouted, pushing the boy in return. The two started to tussle.

"Children, do not fight." The deep voice of the priest, strong yet soothing, quickly ended the disagreement. "We are lucky to have Abuela to tell us stories each week. We need to be grateful for each story she offers us, whether about foxes, boxes or children who know how to behave."

A few adults smiled and nodded in agreement.

The old woman smiled. "I will tell you a story about boxes next time," she said.

Her announcement was greeted with another round of enthusiastic clapping from the young girl, as well as more eye-rolling from the boy.

"What stories has Abuela told this week?" Miguel said into Paige's ear. She jumped.

"Sneaking up on people again, I see," Paige said.

"I was driving through town and saw your rental car. Besides, I like to stop by and listen to her when I can. She was like a mother to us after we lost our parents. Ana and I could always go to her for advice. Or other important things, like ice cream."

Paige noted the grin on Miguel's face.

"You must have been a comfort to her, too" Paige said. "Luz told me she lost a son when he was young."

"Yes, long before I was even born," Miguel said. "Sometimes she tells a story about a snake that took a boy away. It upsets her. We all know what she means, but she will not talk about it, if you ask. What was she talking about today? That trickster, Coyote?"

"Nothing about coyotes," Paige said. "Today was about a bird and his broken wing. And about how a rabbit lost his tail."

"Next week is a story about boxes!" Paige looked down to see the sweet, young girl from the storyteller's audience skipping by, chattering away to her rag doll.

"I think you mean foxes, *mi hija*," Miguel shouted after the girl before turning back to Paige. "Kids get so confused. Most of our legends have to do with the animal spirits. Not all of them, but many."

"Not this time," Paige said. "She really means boxes. The storyteller said she would tell her a story about boxes next week."

"I do not know of any stories about boxes, but sometimes Abuela makes things up to entertain." Miguel surveyed the crowd, noticed the priest turning in their direction, and said a quick goodbye. "Better get to those chores," he said, leaving Paige as quickly as he'd arrived.

Paige watched Miguel retreat and then turned to the approaching priest.

"Hello, Father," Paige said. "You have a lovely church. I stopped by to listen to your town's storyteller." Paige shook hands with the priest.

"I'm Father John. Padre Juan. And thank you. Yes, Abuela is here every Sunday, telling tales to anyone who lingers after Mass. She has been doing this for decades, relaying legends that have been passed down for generations. Along with some creative side stories of her own, I suspect." The priest smiled as he released Paige's hand and smoothed his cassock. "What brings you to Tres Palomas?"

"Half work and half vacation," Paige replied. "I write a series about the Old West for *The Manhattan Post*. We're featuring southwestern mineral springs, and I was due for some personal time, so it was a good mix."

"You must be staying out at Agua Encantada, then. Wonderful place. Luz works hard to keep it going."

"Yes, it seems like it. That, plus she owns the store here – it's quite a heavy load. At least she has good help from Marisol, Miguel and Ana," Paige said.

"Ah, yes. It's not enough help, but at least it's something." The priest noticed a parishioner approaching and shook Paige's hand again. "I hope to see you again while you're here. And you tell Miguel I look forward to seeing him at Mass soon." The twinkle in the priest's eye told Paige the priest meant his statement as a poke to get Miguel to return to church. It must have been a while since he'd shown up to claim a place in a pew.

Paige returned to her car and drove by Luz's store, finding it stayed closed on Sundays. She circled through the town, as she'd done on her first trip into Tres Palomas, noting again how run down the homes and businesses were. In general, the town wasn't too remote to be inaccessible, but it was far enough off the main drag not to draw as many visitors as it could use. Santa Fe and Taos attracted the majority of visitors to the area, which was understandable since both cities offered a variety of culture, galleries and restaurants.

Agua Encantada was obviously the main draw to Tres Palomas. Resort guests who visited Luz's store were also likely to shop at other businesses in town or to grab a bite to eat at the little bar – what was it called? – on the edge of town. The Coyote Cantina – that was it. Catchy little name.

Although normally Paige didn't go alone to bars in strange towns, her curiosity beat her caution, as it tended to do. She turned her car toward the Coyote Cantina and arrived five minutes later. She recognized the pickup truck in the parking space next to hers as Miguel's. So much for heading back to work after he'd made his fast escape from Padre Juan back at the church. Paige grinned.

As Paige entered the cantina, a few people turned to stare, mostly men sitting at the bar, but also a few from small tables scattered around the room. Some wore jeans and T-shirts, as if on a liquid lunch break from outdoor work. Others were dressed in "church" clothes, but with shirttails pulled out and collars loosened in post-worship style. An older woman in a tight tank top, faded jeans and sandals glanced over as she set two bottles of beer in front of customers at a small table. As she turned away from the table and headed back to the bar, she called out to Paige.

"Come on in. Make yourself at home." Some of the men echoed the bartender; she heard low laughs and a whistle.

"Thanks," Paige muttered, taken aback by the attention of the bar's patrons. Her own outfit for the day – a short skirt and sleeveless, fitted blouse – suddenly felt too revealing. The general atmosphere reminded her why she rarely ventured out to bars.

That whistle got the attention of the remaining customers who hadn't noticed her walk in, including one particularly familiar and delighted face.

"Well, well, look who the armadillo dragged in." Miguel patted the empty barstool next to him. Paige approached, half hesitant and half relieved to have a destination.

"Working hard on those chores?" Paige asked as she slid onto the barstool. She couldn't help herself. He deserved the jab.

"Just getting my vitamins before starting in," Miguel replied, holding up a half-consumed draft beer. He waved the bartender over to get Paige something to drink. "Juanita, this is Paige MacKenzie, a guest at the resort. Also a reporter from New York, so watch what you say around her."

"Oh, honey, you came to the right place if you're looking for dirt about this town!" Juanita exclaimed. "All you have to do is hang out here for a few days and you'll know every secret that has ever been whispered in Tres Palomas. Some secrets will be true and some won't, but you'll hear them all." She tossed a cocktail napkin in front of Paige. "What can I get you?"

"Give her a draft on me," Miguel said.

"Make that coffee," Paige said. She turned her head and gave Miguel a disapproving look. "I'm driving, you know."

"Do not worry, *Sonrisa*, this is my first one," Miguel answered, catching Paige's hint.

Juanita laughed as she set an empty coffee mug on the counter and reached for a half-filled glass pot on a warming tray. "Ah, he's calling you '*Sonrisa*.' He's taken a liking to you." She filled the mug and winked at Miguel. "Watch out for this man. He's broken hearts before."

"Now, now, Juanita. Only a dozen or so. Plus yours, of course." Miguel downed the rest of his beer and asked for another.

Paige smiled at the bantering, sipped her coffee and winced. She had a rapid yearning for a good New York latte.

Or, better yet, one from Jackson Hole. It struck her as odd that one of her first thoughts in a run-down New Mexico bar was of Wyoming. But the attention from the men, Miguel included – or was it Miguel in particular – reminded her of Jake. As flattering as Miguel's attention was, it was her Wyoming cowboy she longed to see. She would call him again when she got back to Agua Encantada. His voice always reassured her when she was on the road and feeling out of her element.

Traveling alone wasn't usually uncomfortable. She preferred it to being on the road with company. She could stop wherever she wanted, set her own time schedule and make sudden detours, such as the one she had just made when she pulled into the Coyote Cantina.

"So this is the local watering hole," Paige said, attempting a second sip of the watered-down coffee.

"That it is, pretty lady." Paige turned her head to see a rough looking man slide onto the bar stool to her left.

"Paige MacKenzie, meet Charlie Whitehorse." Paige glanced back at Miguel and noticed he didn't turn his head toward the newcomer.

Juanita threw another cocktail napkin on the counter, automatically setting a bottle of beer on it. Clearly Whitehorse was a regular. It was also clear that Miguel wasn't thrilled to see him.

"Now, you have both of the town troublemakers here," Juanita said. "That's probably good for a scoop for your newspaper. Otherwise they're nothing but a waste of your time."

"Juanita loves us," Miguel quipped.

"As long as people keep their fists off each other and pay their tabs, I love everyone who walks through that door."

"Spoken like a true businesswoman," Miguel said. "And a mighty fine point, too, about people paying their debts."

Immediately, Paige sensed the tension between the men on either side of her, and she felt uncomfortable sitting in the middle of it. She took another sip of coffee and looked for an excuse to leave. Pulling her cell phone out of a pocket, she glanced at the time and stood up. As she attempted to put money on the counter, Miguel waved it away.

"My treat," he said.

Paige thanked him and turned to the other man. "It was nice meeting you, Charlie Whitehorse."

"Likewise." He lifted his bottle and waved it in the air.

After saying goodbye, Paige left for Agua Encantada.

CHAPTER NINE

The tour bus rolled into the parking lot, pulling up outside the office. One by one, senior citizens filed off the vehicle. Many held purses and bags while they chatted with each other and pointed to various locations around the property, clearly excited. From what Luz had told Paige earlier, the group had been traveling, shopping, staying in cities throughout the southwest and now, thanks to the flooding problem at the Santa Fe accommodations, they were getting an unexpected stay at a mineral springs resort. From their conversations, Paige could tell the tour members felt more of a sense of adventure than disappointment at the changed plans.

She watched the arrival from an armchair in the lobby, where a fresh cup of coffee had been a perfect complement to the notes she was writing up for Susan.

The gathering of the guests was like *The Golden Girls* meets *Grumpy Old Men*. If the new arrivals were under seventy years of age, Paige would have been surprised. Yet they had the perky enthusiasm of a college sorority and fraternity get-together. They were there to have a good time and Paige was certain they planned to make the most of their unexpected detour.

Marisol looked overwhelmed at the front desk, though the guests who were lined up waiting for room assignments were patient and polite. Conversations bubbled between fellow travelers, and Marisol often had to attract the attention of the next person in line, once the previous one walked away with keys.

"I can't wait to get into that mineral water and soak, Martha!" A tall woman with a bouffant hairdo and large, bright orange, clunky earrings spoke to a woman of barely five feet and comparable age – Paige guessed mid-seventies – who mirrored the same excitement.

"You and me both, Sylvia," the second woman said. "Thank heavens I picked up that swimsuit back in Albuquerque. I had no idea I'd be using it, but it was such a good sale. I couldn't pass it up! Here we are, with a perfect excuse to use it."

The woman called Sylvia laughed and rolled her eyes. "Martha, I never head out on a trip without a swimsuit in my suitcase. There's always a chance a hotel might have a hot tub, not to mention one or two handsome widowers sitting around the edge. Never hurts to be prepared."

"You have a point there," Martha agreed with a mischievous smile. She stepped up to the front counter as Marisol called her name, looking back at her friend. "Check out the lobby while I get our keys. Maybe they have some good souvenirs here that I can add to the stash of goodies I'm bringing back to the grandkids."

Paige watched Sylvia wander around the lobby while Martha checked in. Sylvia spent just as much time sizing up her fellow travelers as she did exploring.

"Wonderful place you have here, dear," Sylvia said. It took Paige a moment to realize the woman was speaking to her. And that she'd been mistaken for a staff member.

"Oh, I'm just a guest here," Paige said quickly, "though I agree with you; it's a fabulous place."

"Well you look like you belong here. Have you tried the mineral pools yet? I hear they're great for aching joints." Sylvia massaged her right elbow.

"Yes, I have," Paige said. "And I recommend them highly. Ten minutes in that water just about turned my muscles into butter. I haven't felt that relaxed in a long time."

"That's just what I was hoping to hear." Sylvia smiled.

Martha appeared, two keys dangling from one hand. "Here we go, Sylvia, dear, let the good times roll!" Both women moved to pick up suitcases, but Miguel stepped up and stopped them.

"I will help you with those. Beautiful ladies should not have to carry their own bags," he said as he smiled and looked directly into their eyes. The women giggled with delight at the attention. Silently, Paige gave Miguel a few points for timing and tact.

Miguel looked at one of the keys in Martha's hand and, without saying the casita number out loud, picked up the bags for both women. "Follow me, *senoritas.*" The women giggled again.

In groups of twos and fours, the members of the tour group left the office and headed for their cottages. Miguel returned several times to shuttle additional luggage for other guests.

"That's quite a group for us," Marisol said, looking over the registration sheet. "Twenty-four people spread out over fourteen rooms. We'll have our work cut out for us when they check out."

Paige watched Marisol arrange the signed registration cards, placing each in a bucket, a casita number by each file holder.

"It's great they're out traveling," Marisol added. "I wish my mother would go on a trip sometime, but she works every day, and too hard, at that. We all try to help her, but she is proud and always wants to do things herself. At least she allows Lena to open the store for her now."

"Luz mentioned Lena this morning." Paige said.

"Yes, Lena is new to our town, but she's already been a great help and addition to the resort. She moved here a little while ago and began working at the store two hours each morning so my mother can be here to serve breakfast. She's also trained in massage therapy and comes in now and then to take appointments. Anyway, I know my mother is interested in traveling on tours. This is her home – the resort, the guests and her store. She likes her way of life."

"Your mom grew up here, I take it," Paige said.

"Yes, we all did," Marisol replied. "Most of the townspeople have histories that go back many generations. Some people leave, maybe go off to college, meet someone, or take a job somewhere else. But many stay here. Our roots are here."

The front office door slammed and Miguel wandered in, finished with delivering luggage.

"I am heading into town." Miguel dropped a spare key on the counter. "C14 only wanted one key."

Marisol replaced the key in the drawer. "Did you close up the llama barn?"

Miguel shrugged his shoulders. "I will do it when I get back." Without waiting for a response, he flashed a smile at Paige and left.

"Watch out for him, Paige," Marisol said, shaking her head. "I can tell he's taken a liking to you."

"Don't worry," Paige laughed. "Miguel can flirt with me all he wants, but it's not going to get him anywhere. I'm seeing someone." *At least I think so.*

Marisol smiled. "Someone in New York?"

"No," Paige said. "Someone in Wyoming, which makes it...confusing. It's hard to see each other. I have my job traveling and he has a ranch to take care of."

"I'm sure you'll find a way if you like each other," Marisol said.

"Maybe," Paige said, not feeling as sure as she would have liked. *Yes, maybe.*

CHAPTER TEN

Fresh salsa, melted cheese and chopped cilantro covered the fried eggs that rested on a bed of black beans and corn tortillas on the plate that Luz set before Paige.

"This looks delicious!" Paige said. "I've never seen anything quite like it before. What's it called?"

"It is one of our specialties, *huevos rancheros*." Luz smiled as she cleared dishes from vacated tables. "There's extra salsa on the table."

"Thank you!" Paige lifted the small pottery jug and poured a generous amount of red sauce on top of her eggs before tasting them. Travel had taught her to be open to new experiences, including trying new foods. She wasn't about to make her visit to Agua Encantada an exception to that rule.

As Miguel passed by Paige's table, he laughed and eyed the salsa she'd added to her breakfast. "Ah, Luz's homemade salsa and her famous *huevos rancheros*. You'll be a local in no time at this rate, *Sonrisa*."

"I'll take that as a compliment," Paige said, watching Miguel disappear into the kitchen. She filled her fork with a combination of all the ingredients, including a generous portion of salsa. She took a bite and closed her eyes, savoring the mix of flavors. Just as quickly, her eyes popped open wide as her mouth caught on fire. Grateful to see Miguel had returned with a tall glass of water, she ignored the smirk on his face and gulped down the cool beverage.

Miguel took a seat across the table from Paige and waited for her to catch her breath. "I can bring out some sliced jalapeños for you to add, too, if you would like." He sat back in the chair, stretched both arms over his head and then dropped them behind his neck. His grin remained.

"Very funny," Paige said. After several gulps of water, she could breathe again. Miguel reached for a glass pitcher at the end of the table and refilled her glass when she set it down. She shot him a look of surrender and chugged the second glass.

"Now that you can speak again, what do you think?" Miguel asked.

"Powerful but delicious. Are you having breakfast?" Paige scraped some of the salsa to the side and took a much more cautious bite.

"No, I ate earlier," Miguel said. "I have errands to run and resort chores – repairing a fence behind the back row of casitas and then, later, attending to the llamas – your sweetheart, Rico, included."

"Again, very funny," Paige took another sip of water, this one less desperate.

Miguel drummed his hands against the table and then stood up, refilling Paige's water glass one more time. With a grin, he pushed the cold water closer to her place setting and left.

Shortly after Miguel left, Sylvia and Martha entered the breakfast room. They greeted other tour group guests as they passed tables, finally sitting across from Paige. Each wore a jogging suit, Martha's teal, Sylvia's navy blue. Paige noticed Sylvia wore a pin that looked like Ana's design of the three silver doves. It made her plain sweatshirt almost elegant. Luz brought two more breakfast plates to the table and returned to the kitchen.

"Good morning, dear," Sylvia said to Paige. Martha nodded a wordless greeting.

"Good morning to you, as well, ladies," Paige said. She then lowered her voice and whispered across the table. "A word of warning…that salsa in the small pitcher is almost deadly. Delicious, but deadly."

"It's just a matter of moderation," Sylvia said, pouring just a few drops of salsa on her meal. Martha nodded, taking the pitcher from her traveling partner and applying the same amount. Then Sylvia added a few more drops, then Martha did. They repeated the sequence one more time. *Are they trying to one-up each other?* Paige wondered. She watched the ladies take bites, sigh in momentary appreciation and then reach rapidly for the water. Paige was ready to refill their glasses when they put them down.

"I take it the salsa was a bit much for you, too," Sylvia said, laughing when she could breathe again.

"Yes, I learned the same way and someone rescued me by supplying the water." Paige pointed her fork at the last few bites of eggs. "Don't miss out on the meal, though. With just a touch of that salsa, it's delicious."

"Was it the handsome young man who carried our bags for us yesterday? He seems like the type to rescue a lady, doesn't he, Martha?" Martha nodded. "I saw him leaving as we came in. He's a looker, that one," Sylvia continued.

"I suppose," Paige said. It hadn't escaped her that Miguel was easy on the eyes, but with her heart two states away, she saw him more as a source for her article on the resort than anything else.

"Fresh melon slices?" Luz's voice broke Paige's train of thought.

"Yes!" all three women answered simultaneously. "Thank you, Luz," Paige said. She cut a bit piece of honeydew melon and found the fruit immediately soothing to her palate after the spicy salsa.

"Sylvia," Paige said, setting her plate aside and leaning back in her chair. "I see you're wearing a piece of jewelry from the gift shop here. Did you do some shopping last night after settling in?"

Sylvia glanced down at the silver pin and looked back up, perplexed. She tilted her head to the side and looked at Paige.

"No, I haven't had a chance to look in the gift shop, though I want to." Martha nodded in agreement. "I picked this up somewhere along the interstate. Pretty, don't you think?"

"Yes," Paige agreed. "It's beautiful." She bent forward to get a better look, almost certain the design was Ana's. The image of three doves matched others she had seen in Luz's shop. "Did your tour bus stop in Tres Palomas on the way here? Maybe you bought it at Luz's store in town. She sells all sorts of original and authentic artwork, including some jewelry that looks a lot like your pin."

"We came straight here," Martha said.

"Yes," Sylvia said. "Our bus drove in from Albuquerque. Before that we were in Flagstaff. But we stopped along the way a lot, you know, at travel plazas or other places for restroom breaks and to stretch our legs."

"Do you know the name of the shop where you bought it?" Paige asked. "It's such a unique piece."

"Oh, I have no idea," Sylvia said. "That whole stretch of highway had trading post style shops, practically one at every exit once we entered New Mexico." Sylvia took another sip of water and then paused. "And it may look like a unique design, but there were dozens of them at that shop."

"Dozens of similar designs?"

Sylvia shook her head. "No, I mean dozens of that exact design. I didn't care. I doubt anyone at my garden club in Indiana is going to show up wearing the same piece. I just liked it, so I bought it. Gotta have souvenirs, you know. Plus it wasn't expensive, was it, Martha?"

Martha shook her head. "No, it wasn't expensive."

"I think I paid eighteen dollars for it, something like that," Sylvia said. "Isn't that right, Martha? Yes, I think so." Sylvia turned back toward Paige before Martha had a chance to answer. "Pretty reasonable, don't you think, dear?"

"Yes, very reasonable." Paige said. *Too reasonable.*

"I like to buy something on each tour, some sort of authentic souvenir of the area," Sylvia continued. "I have quite a collection at home, including a sweetgrass basket from Charleston and a voodoo doll from New Orleans."

"You didn't buy that alligator head in Florida, though," Martha piped up.

"Of course not," Sylvia sputtered. "That would have given me nightmares. "But I picked up a poker chip in Las Vegas. And don't forget that kitchen tile from the pottery factory in Pennsylvania."

"It sounds like quite a collection," Paige commented. "Helps you remember those trips, I bet."

"Indeed it does!" Sylvia exclaimed.

"What about you, Martha?" Paige turned her attention to the other senior.

"Well, now," Martha paused a moment, mulling over the thoughts. "I did buy some Ghirardelli chocolate in San Francisco."

"I'm not sure that counts as a collection, unless you kept it," Paige pointed out, smiling. "And I suspect you didn't."

"Didn't even make it onto the bus," Sylvia laughed. "Though I admit to helping myself to a few pieces when she wasn't looking, so Martha's not responsible for those – dark chocolate with raspberry, I believe."

"So that's where they went!" Martha tried to frown, but failed. It was clear the women were longtime friends.

Paige smiled. She stood, set the cloth napkin down and pushed her chair in. "I think it's a good day for another soak in those mineral pools."

"We might see you there," Sylvia said. "Don't you think so, Martha?"

Martha nodded, and the three of them left the breakfast room, scattering to their respective casitas to prepare for the day.

CHAPTER ELEVEN

Paige slipped on her swimsuit, followed by shorts, a T-shirt and sandals. Closing the door to her casita, she stepped into the courtyard and looked up at the sky. The white clouds against a deep blue background were a welcome sight after the dark gray ones that had plagued the area the last few days. The howling wind of the first night was a distant memory now, replaced with a soft morning breeze.

Breakfast had given Paige the energy to reorganize her notes. And her conversation with Sylvia and Martha had kicked her curiosity into high gear. Sylvia's story about buying her pin along the interstate didn't sit right since the piece so closely resembled Ana's designs. Intent on combining a little relaxation with research, Paige headed for the spa building.

Halfway to the pools, she paused to pull her ringing cell phone out of her bag.

"How's everything going in New Mexico? Are you managing to stay out of trouble?"

The sound of Jake's voice made Paige smile, as did his teasing question.

"Everything's fine," Paige laughed. "I'm heading to the pools to soak up some of those healthy minerals in the water here. I had breakfast with Sylvia and Martha earlier and just finished going over some notes."

"Sylvia and Martha?"

"They're with a tour group that came in yesterday. Nice women, a couple of characters, must be in their seventies, at least."

"Well, that should keep you safe, hanging out with them," Jake said. "I doubt they'll be dragging you off into any unexpected adventures."

"Actually, there was something unusual I noticed during the meal, something puzzling. Sylvia was wearing a pin that looks exactly like one of Ana's designs."

"And who is Ana?"

"The girl who manages the spa, Miguel's sister."

"And Miguel? Who is Miguel?"

"He's the property manager who gave me the tour that first day, remember? I told you I was about to take a tour. Anyway, his sister, who works in the spa, also makes jewelry, exquisite, one-of-a-kind pieces. I bought some at a store in Tres Palomas." Paige said.

"OK, what's so puzzling about this?" Jake asked. "They probably have a gift store, most resorts do. The guest might have bought it there."

"Well, that's what I thought, but she said she bought it along the Interstate at some trading post. I'd gotten the impression that Ana only sells her jewelry at the resort or at a store in Tres Palomas."

"Maybe this Sylvia is confused," Jake suggested. "About where she bought the pin."

"Maybe," Paige admitted, continuing her walk across the courtyard. "But I still want to ask Ana where she sells her jewelry. I'm planning on relaxing at the spa today, anyway. What about you, how's your day going?"

"Just getting ready to work on one of the smaller cabins, replacing some floorboard," Jake said. "And I've got a broken window on the back side of the barn."

"Your place is going to be in tip-top shape when you get done with all these repairs." Paige paused, hit by a yearning to see the Jackson Hole ranch again, as well as its owner.

Jake either read her unspoken thoughts or mirrored them. "Well, you just might have to come back soon to see the results."

Paige smiled to herself, but didn't respond to the "almost" invitation. After a few casual words of good-bye, she ended the call, slipped the cell phone back in her bag, and stepped into the spa.

Ana looked up as Paige entered. A fresh arrangement of goldenrod and Indian paintbrush filled a glass vase on the end of the counter. The familiar scent of eucalyptus filled the spa's entry hall. The sense of being safe and separated from the outside world returned.

"A quiet day today?" Paige asked.

"It is our Whisper Zone," Ana pointed out. "So, yes, it is quiet. But still busy."

"I'm sure the tour group is keeping you on your toes." Paige knew by the smile Ana returned that she was right. She accepted a bathrobe and slipper bundle from Ana and started toward the pool entrance, then paused. Looking down, she saw a sketchpad and pencil on Ana's side of the counter, several designs roughly drawn on the page.

"Ana, your designs are so unique. I think they'd do well in upscale boutiques and art galleries. Do you sell them other places, outside of Tres Palomas?"

Ana shook her head. "Not outside of town. I have some in our resort gift shop and others in Luz's store, but not anywhere else. It is enough to keep up with the visitors who come through. I would rather spend time on one piece and feel proud of it than to make more without giving them all of my attention."

"Has anyone ever asked you about making larger quantities?"

"Now and then someone suggests it. But it would be more than I could do myself and I do not want to hire others to help. I like that I can do this on my own. And I like them to be unique."

"It makes me happy to hear you say that," Paige said. "For so many other people, making things seems to be about quantity and money these days."

"I am happy with my life as it is. When someone buys a piece, it's the only one like it; I know I have given that person a little bit of myself. And, with it, I get to travel."

"I never thought about art that way," Paige said. "Part of you goes where the art goes."

"Yes, that is exactly right." Ana turned to the door as Sylvia and Martha entered. Both had wrapped their hair in scarves and were dressed in muumuus, loose and brightly colored. Sylvia was not wearing her pin.

Exchanging hellos with Paige, the women soon had robe and slipper bundles in their arms and were headed for the dressing room. Paige lingered a few minutes with Ana.

"Ana, I have one other question. Are you the only one with a key to this building?" Paige was sorry she'd asked as soon as she saw the worry on Ana's face. Once again curiosity had caused her to stick her foot in her mouth. It wasn't likely to be the last time, either, but she regretted the discomfort her question had caused.

"No." A frown creased Ana's brow. "Luz and Marisol keep a key in the office. And Miguel has keys to all the buildings, since he handles upkeep and emergency repairs – a pipe bursting, for example, which happened once last winter. Why do you ask?"

"I thought I saw someone near the building during the storm the other night, a shadow moving. I heard a window or door slam shut. I shouldn't have said anything. I'm sorry if I worried you. I just thought…well, obviously I was mistaken." *I know I wasn't mistaken.*

"Were any lights on?"

"No lights," Paige said.

"I do not think it is possible that anyone was in here," Ana said. She paused, as if thinking it over. "No, once I close the spa for the day, it is closed. No one would have any reason to be here afterhours. Marisol does not care much for the spa, and Miguel would just hop the back fence if he felt like taking a late-night soak. He would not even come inside. Besides, nothing was disturbed." Ana looked around, checked below the counter, and then looked back up at Paige. "Nothing is missing. The only things of true value here would be some back stock of my jewelry, which I hide under the counter in a box, and it is all here."

"Well, it was very windy," Paige said. "It had to just be a latch that came loose and caused the banging. And I did see tumbleweeds rolling by, and they looked a lot like people." She switched topics quickly, pointing toward the pool area. "Which way to the soda pool? I soaked in the iron pool last time."

"Are you just planning to soak? I could schedule a massage for you," Ana said. "We have a therapist onsite today."

"Not right now." Paige smiled. "But maybe I'll consider it for later. I haven't had one for a long time."

"The hot stone massage is especially popular," Ana pointed out. "You can add an aromatherapy treatment to make it even better – a combination of orange, anise and chamomile, for example.

"I'll keep that in mind. Meanwhile, the soda pool...."

Ana pointed toward the back door. "Just go out and follow the path around the iron pool. You will see a sign just to the right of a small cactus garden. The soda pool is behind that. You can set your belongings on one of the lounge chairs or tables nearby. Or I can give you a key to a locker, if you prefer."

"Thanks, but I won't need a locker this time," Paige said. "The ladies from the tour group seem fairly harmless and I don't have anything of value with me."

Paige followed Ana's directions, easily finding the soda pool. Dropping her outer clothing and the robe bundle on a lounge chair, she slipped into the water, feeling the warmth surround her shoulders. Resting the back of her neck against the pool's edge, she closed her eyes and let her thoughts wander. If Sylvia's pin looked exactly like Ana's designs, yet Ana only sold in town, what was going on? If someone had bought one of Ana's pieces in Tres Palomas and resold it along the interstate, the price Sylvia paid for it should have been higher than what Ana charged. Yet it was less than half. Plus Sylvia had said there were many of the same design. Maybe someone had gotten hold of a photograph of Ana's work and was making cheap copies. Anyone could have taken a picture while traveling through.

Her thoughts shifted to the events of the first night. In spite of what Ana said, Paige was certain someone had been inside the spa building. Something wasn't right. And Paige was determined to find out what it was.

CHAPTER TWELVE

Charlie Whitehorse cursed as he took a swing at the burly figure in the parking lot of the Tierra Roja Casino. He didn't appreciate the greeting he'd received. Being shoved up against a cement wall and threatened was hardly his idea of a warm welcome. After all the years he'd been a faithful customer, what kind of gratitude was that? And all over a little outstanding balance? What made it even more insulting was the fact he'd arrived with a payment. Five thousand dollars ought to earn a customer something more than a slam against a cement wall.

"Five grand is nothing, Whitehorse. Hector asked for twenty and you're already a week overdue with that. You can add another five to your balance." The menacing figure glared as he spit out the words. "I don't have the patience for this. We run a legitimate business. This kind of ill will spreads rumors. Makes it look like we encourage people to run up debts they can't pay."

"I drove four hours to bring you this money," Whitehorse sputtered. "At least you could show some appreciation. Go hassle someone else. Hector probably has dozens of clients gambling here."

"But *you're* the one who owes the guy money. His other clients pay up faster than you do. *You're* the problem and I'm telling you to take care of business."

"I'll have it soon. I only need another week. He'll have his money." Whitehorse could feel blood trickling down his forehead and along the bridge of his nose.

"You think I'm a fool? You have no idea where you'll get the money and, personally, I don't care how you come up with it. Get it paid, all of it. Or you'll be sorry."

Whitehorse watched the man walk away. Self-righteous jerk, trying to act like the casino didn't encourage customers to spend more than they had. That was exactly what they did. He wouldn't be surprised if the casino was getting a cut of the outrageous interest that Hector was charging. Why else had his bookie kept advancing him money, even though Hector knew Whitehorse was behind in his payments? The casino was probably in cahoots with Hector.

Of course, there was that small side business, too, which had nothing to do with the casino. At least it had started off small. That was before Hector began seeing the money roll in and used some of the profit to lure Whitehorse further into the world of gambling. He wouldn't be surprised if Hector had dozens of side businesses going on. The guy was obviously used to manipulating people for his own benefit. He kept his pawns nearby and hooked, found their weaknesses and set up perfect traps. Like the one that had just caused him to be thrown against a cement wall.

Walking toward the parking garage's elevator, Whitehorse pulled out a bandana from his back pocket and ran it across his face, wincing as he reached the bleeding cut. It didn't feel all that bad, not compared to beatings he'd taken in the past. He knew the difference between a warning and actual punishment and this was definitely just a warning.

A good rinse from the restroom's cold-water faucet and he'd be ready to roll. After all, he still had five hundred dollars in his pocket, and he felt the beginning of a lucky streak. It wouldn't take long to turn that five hundred into five thousand and then turn that into the twenty that would get both the bookie and casino owner off his back.

At times, he'd considered going to another casino to win the money back, but at Tierra Roja, they cut him some slack as long as he was making payments. This only proved that they knew what he knew – his lucky streak was close.

The casino was crowded when he walked in. He'd done a reasonable job of patching up his pummeled face, waiting until the bleeding stopped before heading into the throng of people lined up around tables. They were focused on the games, hypnotized by the hands of the dealers, the cards being drawn and the general atmosphere of excitement. That next big win was right around the corner and they all knew it. And Whitehorse planned to be the one to hit it.

Ordering a scotch and soda from the bar, he leaned against the wall and pulled out a cigarette. Alcohol and nicotine always gave him an edge, an advantage. No one else would believe that, but he knew what helped the cards fall in his favor, just the way he knew this was his lucky day.

Leaving the bar, he cruised the room with his drink in one hand and cigarette in the other. Several tables looked promising, though he quickly eliminated a couple with dealers he didn't care for. It didn't matter that the casino kept cameras on the dealers to keep them honest. He knew a few couldn't be trusted. If they could, he wouldn't have fallen into the debt he had. But that didn't matter on this particular day. Things were about to turn around.

He stopped by an ashtray and put out the cigarette, smashing it into the sandy dish. Now focused, he eliminated the remaining tables one by one. All thoughts of the recent skirmish set aside, a smile spread across his face as he approached the table. This was his lucky day, finally. It was time to buy in.

CHAPTER THIRTEEN

The late afternoon sun cast shadows across the landscape and tinged the pathway to the llama barn with a warm hue. Paige took her time walking, relaxed from the long soak in the soda pool. She had been tempted to take a nap when she'd returned to her room, but her thoughts were moving too quickly. She needed to talk to Miguel.

Rico leaned over the fencing, watching Paige approach. Josie was by the barn door with Miguel, who was adjusting some type of saddle on the llama's back.

"Don't spit at me, ok?" Paige whispered to Rico. She paused, waiting for a response. No spitting. Satisfied they'd reached an understanding, she turned toward Miguel.

"Are you planning to ride her?" Paige winced as soon as the words left her mouth. Llamas were not horses, and she knew perfectly well they weren't for riding. The saddle obviously served to hold a pack full of supplies. "I mean take her somewhere, of course."

Miguel glanced at Paige, amused, then looked back at Josie. "No, we do not ride them, which I suspect you already know. But if the weather holds up, some of the tour members want to take a llama trek tomorrow during lunch. We load up the llamas with food and head out on a hike. I am inspecting the saddle to be sure it is in good shape. Guests can take turns holding the llama's lead as they walk. There is a good, shady spot for a picnic about a mile up the trail."

"It sounds like fun," Paige admitted.

"It is," Miguel said, checking the straps of the llama's saddle. "The trail winds uphill, but just a little. They can handle it. The vistas from the picnic area are excellent." He paused to look at Paige. "You should join us."

"Maybe I will. Is Rico going, too?"

Miguel laughed. "I see I have some tough competition. He might. If we only have a few group members going, Josie can handle it. If more go, Rico will join us, too." Miguel paused. "Of course, if it means you will go, I am sure Rico will be happy to accompany you."

"I'll see," Paige said, tempted. "Meanwhile, I came down here to ask you about something odd." She glanced over her shoulder to make sure no one was behind her, listening. Miguel picked up on her hesitance to speak up and walked closer.

"What is it?" Miguel leaned an elbow against the fence and looked at Paige, a hint of a smile crossing his smooth, tanned face. He reminded her of the subjects of print ads in menswear catalogs – casual, posed perfection with a southwestern, outdoor flair. He was using the pretext of listening as a means of flirting.

"Sylvia was wearing a silver pin at breakfast this morning that looked a lot like one of Ana's."

"Who is Sylvia?" Miguel now seemed like a man who was about to hear a story that didn't interest him, but he would listen out of politeness.

"One of the tour group ladies. You carried her baggage to her room last night."

"OK. It sounds like she found a pin in the gift shop that she liked, or bought it at Luz's store." Raising his eyebrows, he stepped back, his voice growing animated. "Which brings to mind something I never thought of before: we could bribe the bus drivers to stop there when they come through. I did not think of this before, but…"

"Miguel!" Paige stomped her foot to make him focus. She crossed her arms, impatient.

"Sorry," Miguel said, returning to his previous position against the fence. "Go on."

"She didn't buy the pin here. Not in the lobby's gift shop and not at Luz's store."

"How do you know?" Miguel shifted his weight, more attentive than before.

"I asked her, of course!" Paige threw her arms out to the sides, palms up, exasperated.

"Then it is someone else's design," Miguel said, his tone matter of fact. "Ana is hardly the only jewelry artist around. There are hundreds of artists and thousands of designs. I suppose the next thing you will tell me is that the pin is silver with turquoise stones. That would certainly narrow it way down."

"No need to be sarcastic. But, as a matter of fact.…" Paige started.

Miguel laughed, turning away to head back to Josie, who was munching on a bale of hay.

"It was a silver design with three doves," Paige shouted at his retreating figure. He stopped and turned back to face her.

"Three doves?"

"Yes, three silver doves, with an abstract line underneath that looks like water," Paige said. "And don't act like I don't know what I'm talking about. I've visited Luz's store and looked over the pieces in the resort gift shop, not to mention talking to Ana about her artwork when I was at the spa. And I'm telling you this was one of her designs."

Miguel leaned against the fence again, far less composed and looking nothing like a magazine ad this time. "But you said the guest did not buy it here. So where did she say she bought it?"

Paige shrugged. "She doesn't remember. Said one of those shops along the Interstate, at a travel plaza where they found a trading post or something."

"On Interstate 40, hours from here? That is impossible," Miguel said. "Ana has never sold her jewelry to other stores, only to individual customers here or in town. Maybe the guest is confused. Or...she might have bought it in Santa Fe...."

"Santa Fe?" Paige asked.

"Never mind," Miguel said quickly. "Go on."

"Well, she didn't buy it in Santa Fe," Paige insisted. "She'd remember if she did. Besides, didn't you just say Ana doesn't sell her designs outside of Tres Palomas?"

Paige watched Miguel shift his weight uneasily.

"Anyway, there's one more thing," Paige said, ignoring Miguel's change in behavior for now.

"What is that?"

"Sylvia said there were dozens of pins at the shop that were identical."

Miguel had begun pacing at this point. "That does not make sense."

Both Paige and Miguel fell silent for a minute. Josie smacked one hoof against the ground. Rico let out a sound that resembled a cross between a foghorn and a snort.

"Look," Paige said, "I'll see if she has a receipt. I can tell her I want to call the store to get one for myself or for a present for someone. I'll make up some excuse. Then we can find out if I'm wrong, and I probably am. Honestly, I didn't mean to worry you. I just wondered where else Ana might be selling her pieces."

Miguel looked around at the llamas and put both hands on his hips. "I have to get these guys fed and put them in the barn before it gets dark. Maybe Sylvia will wear the pin to dinner. You can notice it again and ask about the receipt," Miguel said.

"Maybe Ana will be at dinner and see the pin herself," Paige suggested, wondering why this hadn't occurred to her before.

"Ana does not dine with the guests. Once she closes the spa, she goes home to work on jewelry. But I will be there. Luz is serving chile rellenos. I never miss that."

"Is that the same chile that you made me pour all over my eggs this morning? If so, I'm not falling for it this time." Paige placed her hands on her hips.

Miguel laughed. "That was salsa and I did not make you pour it on your eggs. You did that all on your own, willingly."

"You didn't warn me," Paige pointed out.

"I made sure you had water. Anyway, chile rellenos are delicious, you will see. And you will not need to pour any salsa on top. It will already be on there."

"Oh, in that case I feel much better now."

"You said no sarcasm, remember?"

"Unless it's deserved." Paige turned away and started back to the casita.

CHAPTER FOURTEEN

Charlie Whitehorse cursed as he swerved into the bumpy driveway, narrowly missing the roadside stand that sat at the front of his property. As much as he wouldn't mind running the booth down, it was still his best hope for getting out of trouble. As long as he could stay a few steps ahead of Hector, he'd be fine.

He parked his truck alongside the small trailer at the end of the driveway, stepping out and slamming the door. What was he going to do now? He'd handed over almost every dollar he could get his hands on to Hector's henchman. But he owed much more. And the extra five hundred he hadn't turned over in the parking garage – lost at the casino.

He kicked a truck tire and let a few more expletives fly. He'd been so sure this was his lucky night. He'd followed all the patterns that helped him win other times, respected each superstition, engaged in every practiced habit. None of it had helped, not this time. Not the last ten times, for that matter.

The trailer was dark when he stepped inside, but lit up with a quick flip of a switch. It was one advantage to a nine by twelve foot space. It didn't take much to light it up. He dropped the truck keys on a cracked counter and picked up a single key on a chain at the same time. Throwing the door open, he headed outside again and continued down the driveway until he reached a metal storage shed that was at least five times the size of his trailer. Now, that would be a more reasonable living space, he'd often thought. But the trailer would never hold as much as the storage shed, so he couldn't switch. In any case, it wasn't his choice. Everything was up to Hector, which made it all the more maddening.

Sure, he'd had problems with gambling in the past, not to mention being under Hector's blackmailing thumb for longer than he could remember. But his whole life had been turned upside down when the trading post and storage shed came into play. Until then, he'd enjoyed the small trailer and empty lot of land that he'd bought when he was younger. It was the one place he could be alone when he wanted to. He didn't bother anyone and no one bothered him. But once the roadside stand and storage shed were built, his peaceful retreat went down the drain.

He fumbled with the padlock, dropping the key in the dirt twice. He patted the ground with both hands in order to find it each time. After the third time, he got it unlocked. He removed the padlock, stuck the key in his pocket and rolled the sliding metal door aside just enough to step into the unit. He picked up the flashlight he kept just inside and turned it on, moving the beam around the room.

As he'd expected, a new stack of boxes sat not far from the door. The delivery had come in. At least that was good news. The turnaround time was improving and so were his chances of getting out of trouble; at least he could hope so. For now, it was just a matter of damage control. That and trying to stay alive. Who knew how many goons Hector had and what they were capable of? That little roughing up at the casino was nothing.

Whitehorse ran the flashlight's beam across the interior of the storage unit, detesting the careful stacks of boxes. A worktable held trays of goods and packaging supplies. Two wooden stools sat alongside the table. It wasn't much, but the shabby building filled its purpose. Or Hector's purpose, more accurately.

He never should have let Hector get more control of him. The gambling loans had been bad enough. But when faced with what sounded like a way out, he fell for it. He should have known it sounded too good to be true: a short-term business deal and a clean slate when it was all over. His debts would be paid off and the threats he'd lived with for decades would stop. What a fool he'd been. Now not only was he still in debt, he was stuck in the middle of someone else's illegal business dealings. In addition, he was deceiving Miguel, who was a good guy. When it came right down to it, he was deceiving everyone around him. The only one he wasn't deceiving was himself, but there was nothing he could do about it. He was in way too deep.

Closing the door to the storage building, he padlocked it and returned to the trailer. Hector's workers would be there in the morning. He'd be back in Tres Palomas, where Hector left him alone, aside from a threatening or demanding phone call now and then. That was the one part of their bargain that Hector had always honored. And for a few days he could pretend the whole mess didn't even exist.

CHAPTER FIFTEEN

Paige brushed her hair back off her face and wrapped an elastic band around it, tightening it into a high ponytail. It wasn't her usual hairstyle, but Agua Encantada had adjusted her mood. She couldn't pinpoint exactly what was different, but felt it, nonetheless. She was calmer, yet more energized, relaxed, yet more curious about her surroundings. It was as if she were growing inward and outward at the same time, something her editor would tell her was far too poetic for a reporter.

The magic of the area had bewitched her, setting off that vacation phenomenon that causes a person to dress differently, even speak differently at times. Could someone take on a persona of a geographic area? That was what this felt like. She was no longer a New York City girl, but a chameleon with a southwestern flair.

Twisting her head from side to side, she contemplated the simple silver hoop earrings that she was wearing. As pleasant as they appeared in the mirror, they were too drab for her newly discovered spirit. Even her new earrings with the three doves were tame for her mood. She'd have to return to Luz's store, where she could pick up another pair of earrings, one of Ana's more exotic designs. Something with coral and malachite, maybe, something that dangled – that would be good. She could buy a peasant blouse with ruffled sleeves at the same time, maybe a style that could sit just off her shoulders. Thinking of this newly manufactured image of herself, she smiled, grabbed a sweater and headed to the resort café.

Several of the tour group members were already dining when she entered, filling all the seats but one at their table. Sylvia was not among them. She didn't see Miguel, either, but chose a different table with room for him. From the way his face lit up earlier when he mentioned the chile rellenos, she was certain he'd show up. And as Marisol slid the plate of food in front of her, she could see why. Dripping with melted cheese and salsa, the aroma alone brought on a rush of hunger. She eyed the heaping side servings of rice and beans and immediately began to justify carb loading. The llama trek, for example, would require energy. And she was on a semi-vacation, after all. Surely she could hit the floor and do a few sit-ups after it was over and no harm would be done.

"This looks fabulous," Paige said, looking up. "How spicy is it...?" Marisol smiled and glanced over Paige's shoulder.

"Not spicy at all." Miguel slid into the chair beside her. "You are going to have to toughen up to survive this trip of yours, you know." He pointed at his place setting with both index fingers, shooting a manipulative but sweet look to Marisol.

"I'm tough enough," Paige protested. She startled as the door of the café slammed closed. She leaned forward, looking around Miguel to see that several more tour group members had entered. They took a table on the other side of the café. Sylvia and Martha had not yet arrived. She eased back in her chair and contemplated her meal.

"Poblano chiles are mild," Miguel said, rubbing his hands together as Marisol emerged from the kitchen and set a matching plate in front of him. "And if you insist on being a wimp, you can just dig out the melted cheese from inside."

"There's more cheese inside?" Paige was already setting up a fitness routine in her head. Twenty minutes on the treadmill, twenty minutes on a stair master and a solid hour in spin class. That should do it, for half of the meal, anyway.

"Here," Miguel said, sliding a basket of sopaipillas in her direction. "You can soak up the extra sauce and cheese with these. Best bread you will ever have."

"You're no help at all," Paige said, mentally adding some jump roping to her workout.

This time when the café door opened, Sylvia and Martha entered. Paige tapped Miguel's arm to get him to notice the two women and knocked a huge bite of relleno off his fork and back onto his plate.

"What?" he said. He stabbed his relleno again.

"Miguel! Pay attention!" Paige whispered. "That's Sylvia, the one who said she bought Ana's pin out of town. See the woman in the turquoise blouse?"

Miguel set down his fork and looked toward the front door. "She is not wearing any jewelry."

"No," Paige sighed. "You're right, she's not. But she was earlier."

Impulsively, Paige stood up and waved across the room for Sylvia and Martha to join them. They were soon seated at the table with Paige and Miguel, dinner plates in front of them. Paige took a drink of water in preparation for whatever degree of spice lay ahead.

"Thank you for saving us," Sylvia said. "I really didn't want to sit at that other table."

Martha leaned forward and whispered, "One of the single members of our group has the hots for Sylvia."

Paige choked on her water, setting the glass down quickly. She could see Miguel grinning out of the corner of her eye. "Is that so?"

"Oh, I suppose he's interested," Sylvia admitted. "He was on the last tour I took, to the Panama Canal." She took a bite of chile relleno and closed her eyes, sighing in satisfaction.

"Wouldn't leave her alone," Martha whispered, glancing over her shoulder as if sharing a top government secret.

"Is he by himself on this trip?" Paige looked over at the other table, noticing the empty chair beside one of the men.

"Yes," Martha said. "On this trip and the last one, too. He was widowed about a year ago, I think."

Paige reached for the basket of sopaipillas and offered them to both ladies. "Maybe he's just lonely, Sylvia, and looking for someone to talk to."

"Oh, don't you believe that," Martha giggled. "You know how men are. Always wanting a few benefits, if you know what I mean." Impishly, she wiggled her eyebrows.

This time Miguel choked, much to Paige's delight.

"Sylvia," Paige said, changing the subject. "You're not wearing that beautiful pin you had on earlier today. I was thinking about it after I saw you. I need a gift for an aunt and would love to pick up one for her. Have you remembered where you bought it?"

Sylvia shook her head. "No, I don't know. We stopped at so many places."

"Maybe it was that shop we stopped at when Gertrude needed to use the restroom," Martha suggested.

"No," Sylvia said, tearing off a piece of sopaipilla and putting it in her mouth.

"Or that other stop, when Ruby needed to go," Martha offered.

Sylvia swallowed and turned to face her friend. "Martha, the bus driver had to stop for one person or another at every restroom on I-40! This is not going to help me remember where I bought the pin."

"That's OK," Paige said quickly. "If you happen to remember later, I'd love to know."

CHAPTER SIXTEEN

Paige glanced over her shoulder as she paused on the trail. Miguel was twenty yards back, moving down the path, handing a water bottle to each of the nine guests who'd signed up for the llama trek. He took his time with each one, exchanging a few friendly words. He was good for the resort; she could see that now. He could charm guests of any age. Seeing Sylvia and Martha blush when he handed them their water bottles proved that.

They'd been fortunate with the weather. Though the sun shone strongly, the day was relatively cool. The exercise was challenging enough for the group without adding in high temperatures. Miguel had planned the trip to cover only half its normal length, avoiding a steeper portion of terrain.

Paige reached over and patted her hiking companion on the shoulder, getting a huff of appreciation in return.

"It's just the two of us, Rico. We're the leaders."

"Hey, do not forget Josie, she is carrying half the lunch supplies," Miguel said, coming up from the rear.

Josie didn't look at all offended. She was busy nibbling at the leather harness of her saddle pack.

"How are Sylvia and Martha doing?" Paige couldn't help worrying about the senior group. In spite of the shorter hiking plan, it was still a good deal of exercise. Even she felt a little short of breath, not that she was about to admit it.

"Fine," Miguel said. "This is our third stop and the picnic area is just ahead. They will be rested before we head back down. Any more word about the pin that looked like Ana's?"

"No," Paige answered. "I asked Sylvia again right before we left the llama barn. She has no idea where she bought it. It sounds like they stopped at every trading post between Flagstaff and Albuquerque. That could be dozens of places."

Paige looked out at the vista from their location on the trail. Tall cactus dotted the landscape, separated by low bursts of sagebrush and occasional splatters of red and gold flowers. Sparse, but gorgeous, she thought. It was so different from Wyoming and Montana, but beguiling in its own way.

"Maybe she just purchased it here, Miguel," Paige said. "Sylvia could be confused about where she bought it. Obviously she doesn't remember."

"Maybe," Miguel said, his tone unconvinced. "Or maybe someone is selling Ana's pieces without her permission. You know, reselling them for a profit."

Miguel swatted Josie's rear end, to get her to move along. Paige copied him, and Rico started walking right away.

"Well, it's not illegal to resell merchandise," Paige pointed out as they moved forward. "Free enterprise and all that."

"True," Miguel acknowledged.

"But...sell them for less than they paid for them? That doesn't make sense," Paige added.

"Also true. Unless they just needed the money. Sometimes people get desperate and sell for whatever they can get."

Miguel pointed to a clearing up ahead with several rustic benches set apart from the trail. As they approached the area, they pulled the llamas aside and waited for the guests to catch up. Miguel pulled blankets from Rico's pack and spread them across the benches. "We usually use this as a resting point, but today we will stop for lunch here and then turn back."

Paige watched Miguel pull a bag from Josie's pack, distributing sandwiches to some of the guests. Paige helped herself to a second bag and did the same.

"You *are* a guest, you know." Sylvia and Martha smiled as they took sandwiches from her. "You should sit and enjoy lunch."

"I feel restless doing nothing," Paige said.

When she looked up from her small task, she noticed that Miguel had walked down the trail thirty yards or so away from his charges. Odd. She saw Whitehorse waiting for him.

She turned her attention back to the tour members. "I'm not used to just sitting around."

"Sometimes sitting is the best thing to do, youngster," Sylvia said.

"That's right," Martha said.

Outnumbered, Paige took the last sandwich and sat down, watching Miguel from a distance. The conversation between the two men had grown animated. Although she couldn't hear what they were saying, both gestured angrily with their arms.

By the time Miguel returned to the group, the last of the lunch meal was consumed.

"I am sorry for stepping away, ladies and gentlemen. I hope you enjoyed your lunch."

Several group members declared that restrooms would be a good idea, so Miguel reloaded Rico and Josie's packs and began the hike back to the resort. Paige kept step with Miguel.

"Are you OK?" she asked.

"Of course. Why do you ask?" He looked at the path ahead and not at Paige as he spoke.

"You looked upset while you were talking to Whitehorse," Paige said.

"He should not have interrupted my work. But it is nothing for you to worry about."

"All right then." Paige patted Rico and dropped the subject.

Once they reached the resort, the guests scattered in various directions and Miguel returned the llamas to the barn. Paige headed for her casita to shower off the trail dust. Despite the pleasant afternoon, a few things bothered her: the origin of Sylvia's pin, the break-in at the spa her first night, and the unsettling interaction between Miguel and Whitehorse that afternoon. Her instincts told her something was wrong. And those instincts were usually right.

Twenty minutes later, she stood by the window, towel-drying her hair and soaking in the late afternoon sun as it flowed into the room. Tossing her towel over the back of a chair, she picked up her phone and dialed Jake's number.

"A llama trek?"

Paige smiled at the sound of Jake's voice. It made her casita feel a little less lonely. Or perhaps it felt more so, now that she thought about it. She hated that she was too far away to see him.

"Yes, a llama trek and picnic," Paige said. "Miguel was taking some of the seniors out, so I went along. You should see the scenery from up on the trail, Jake. It's breathtaking, completely different from Jackson Hole, but enchanting in a whole different way."

"That's nice," Jake said. His voice was suddenly devoid of enthusiasm. "How's the article coming? Have you found time to do your work?"

Paige removed the phone from her ear and looked at it, confused. It was Jake, no question, but it didn't sound like him at all now. She placed the phone back against her ear.

"The article's coming along fine. But remember, I'm also here on vacation. So I'm trying to take advantage of resort activities. Plus, getting involved will help me write a more authentic article." Why was she even justifying her actions? What was really going on in this conversation?

"Jake?" Paige waited for a response, but heard only silence. "Jake, is something wrong? This doesn't even sound like you."

"I'm just..." Jake paused before continuing. "I'm just stressed about some ranch business. It's nothing, really."

Paige heard the sound of shuffling papers start up in the background, but didn't buy the excuse. Something else was bothering him, but trying to pry it out wasn't going to work. Ignoring his strange attitude, she continued on.

"Anyway, we took Josie and Rico up to a picnic area with nine guests from the senior tour group."

"We?" Jake's tone was flat.

"Yes, Miguel and...." *Aha!* Paige had to fight to not laugh out loud. *Seriously?* She opened her mouth to respond and then closed it again. Why should she have to defend herself? She'd done nothing wrong. For one thing, nothing but casual friendship was going on with Miguel. And for another, the nature of her relationship with Jake wasn't clear. This was one of the problems with the long distance situation. It was hard to define when their time together was so limited. As the implications of Jake's cool attitude set in, she felt less flattered by his jealousy and more annoyed by his lack of trust.

"Paige...?"

"Maybe we should just talk later." Paige had no desire to argue and, whether Jake was headed in that direction or just letting insecurities get the best of him, patience had never been one of her virtues. It would be wiser to end the call than to let it evolve into a confrontation.

"Fine."

"I'll call you tomorrow," Paige said, avoiding the obvious: she could call him that night, if she wanted to. At the moment, she didn't.

"Fine," Jake repeated. The sound of rustling papers resumed, just another reminder of the ranch life that she wasn't a part of.

Paige ended the call and tossed her cell phone on the bed. She had her own work to do, both for *The Manhattan Post* and for her growing curiosity about everything going on at the resort. She didn't have time to argue. Even if she did, she had no desire to.

CHAPTER SEVENTEEN

The parking lot at Luz's shop was empty when Whitehorse pulled in, aside from Lena's car. This wasn't by chance. He knew exactly when Luz finished serving breakfast at the resort and when she would arrive at the shop. Since Miguel refused to get him any more jewelry, Luz's morning assistant was his best source. She was a perfect solution, at least temporarily, until he could wrangle more out of Miguel. She was honest and naïve enough not to be curious about his motives, yet just materialistic enough to go along with a bit of bribery. In this case, that meant a quick profit. No harm done. He got what he needed, no laws were broken, and she had a few extra bucks in her pocket. That was an advantage of doing business with someone new in town, someone who didn't know his untrustworthy reputation.

Lena was seated behind the sales counter, reading, but smiled when he walked in and stood up to greet him.

"A nice morning out there," she said, pulling out a velvet display tray and setting it on the counter.

"Yes, it is," Whitehorse answered. "And an even better one if you have something new for me today."

"Of course I do," Lena said, indicating the display. At least a dozen pieces of jewelry were arranged on the tray. Most were pins of varying designs, with a few sets of earrings and pendants mixed in. "Your Santa Fe customers ought to like this new piece of Ana's, don't you think?" She lifted up a silver cactus pin with several flowers of inlaid coral.

"Nice," Whitehorse said, setting the piece aside. Silently, he sighed. If only he actually had Santa Fe customers to sell it to. At least his lies were consistent. Not as much to keep track of and fewer chances of accidental slips in conversations. "What else?"

"This new pendant is beautiful." Lena held up a small sun design, which swayed from a silver chain.

"A little small for these customers," he said. "They like pieces that are big enough to catch someone's attention." Exactly like he was trying not to do, he thought – catch anyone's attention.

"How about this?" Lena pulled out another tray, indicating a silver galloping horse. Tiny specks of turquoise dotted the horse's mane.

"Yes, definitely that one." Whitehorse set it aside with the cactus pin. "I can use a third today," he said, when Lena paused.

"I don't know. That might seem odd to Luz. I usually only buy one or two, at the most."

Whitehorse leaned forward, looking Lena in the eye. "That's your problem. We have an arrangement. I pay you, you pay the store, and everything's covered. You should be able to sell me ten pieces without a problem."

"The problem is that I'm not wearing the pieces I'm buying," Lena pointed out. "Luz has already mentioned this."

"Do you have another piece, or not?" Whitehorse was losing his patience. "I don't have all day. And you know Luz will be here soon." He glanced at the clock on the shop wall. Lena did the same, looking back at him, resigned.

"How about this one?" She picked up a larger piece from the first tray, a turtle with inlaid stones of lapis, turquoise and malachite.

"Fine." Whitehorse said. "Ring them up." He watched while she entered the items into the cash register. "What's the total today?" he asked.

"Ninety-seven dollars and forty-two cents."

Whitehorse pulled one hundred dollars from his wallet and watched her complete the sale. After she handed him his change, she placed the jewelry in a small bag and held onto it. Whitehorse threw another hundred on the counter and grabbed the bag.

"Keep the change this time," he grumbled. "We are fair and square now, Lena. You bought them from Luz and paid retail. I bought them from you at double that price – that part is our secret. My customers will buy them from me for more than that, so all is good."

Whitehorse returned to his truck, backed out of the parking lot and headed for the cantina. Juanita would be opening soon for the usual lunch customers who somehow survived their workdays on nachos and beer. He couldn't do anything with the new jewelry until later, anyway. Joining the crowd seemed like a good plan.

When he arrived, Juanita was just swinging the door of the Coyote Cantina open. She looked up, nodded her head and went back inside, leaving the door propped open for the customers who were pulling into the parking lot. A sign by the entrance read, "Tuesday Special: Nachos and a Draft - $6." With draft refills at just two dollars, almost everyone in town would turn up at Juanita's at some point on any given Tuesday. On one hand, that meant he might run into people he didn't want to see. On the other hand, most people knew they could find him there, anyway, Tuesday or any of six other days.

He shoved the jewelry from Luz's shop into his glove compartment and headed inside, taking what he considered to be his own seat at the bar. Juanita slid his favorite beer in front of him and called in an order to the kitchen for nachos with extra jalapeños.

"You make me feel like I've come home, Juanita," Whitehorse said, wrapping a hand around the beer.

"You should, Whitehorse," Juanita said. "You just about live here." She waved her hand at a group of arriving customers, indicating a side table. She then slapped her hand on the pass-through and called in another order of nachos to the kitchen, this one without jalapeños, but with extra cheese. She grabbed the first order and set it in front of him.

"I gotta hand it to you," Whitehorse said. "You do know your customers."

"Only a fool in business wouldn't." Juanita poured four draft beers and served them to her new customers. Whitehorse watched the old bartender, then turned back to find a hand reaching into his plate of nachos.

"What...? Oh, it's you, of course," Whitehorse grumbled, looking up to see Miguel holding a chip dripping with cheese.

"You must keep your eyes open if you do not want anything stolen." Miguel sat down two stools away, leaving space between them. Leaning forward, he made sure he could still reach the nachos. "Like jewelry, for example."

Whitehorse took a slow drink from his draft. He pulled a jalapeño-covered nacho from his plate and wolfed it down, following it with another slug of beer before speaking.

"My customers are paying up this weekend. You'll have the money then."

"How about I go on up to Santa Fe with you and help collect," Miguel said. "If they are young and attractive, I might have better luck than you."

Whitehorse ignored the snide remark. It had been a long time since he could play Miguel's handsome bachelor game, but that was the least of his problems now.

"I assure you, they're not young and attractive."

Juanita passed by, setting draft refills in front of both men.

"How's that sister of yours doing, Whitehorse?" Juanita said. The question eased the friction in the conversation between the two men.

"Fine, I guess. I don't see her much," Whitehorse said. "Once or twice a week I have dinner with her."

"I saw her a couple days ago," Miguel said, swiping another nacho and grimacing when he took a bite. "What is with all these jalapeños?"

"What's with you stealing my nachos?" Whitehorse pulled the plate out of Miguel's reach. "And just when did you see my sister?"

"It was…Sunday, I think." Miguel paused. "Yes, Sunday, over at St. Bernadette's."

Whitehorse threw his head back and roared with laughter. Even Juanita cracked a smile.

"Miguel, you are so full of it," Whitehorse barked. "You haven't been to Mass since the Macias sisters' confirmation and that was five years ago. Everyone in this town knows Padre Juan has been after you ever since."

"And he only went that time because Luz made him go," Juanita added. "And only because they were her godchildren."

"It'd take a miracle to get you to that church." Whitehorse lifted his beer and shook his head from side to side. Pausing, he added, "Or…something more enticing. A

107

pretty lady, maybe? Like the one who was in here the other day?"

"That's right," Juanita said. "Hate to admit it, but every now and then you're smart, Whitehorse. You mean that reporter from New York."

"Paige," Miguel said. "And even if she is attractive..."

Whitehorse and Juanita mouthed the word "if" to each other.

"...it is not enough to get me inside the church, but I did stop by because I saw her outside the courtyard after Mass had ended."

"You mean when my sister was telling her stories," Whitehorse said. "What silly tales did she tell this week?"

Miguel shrugged his shoulders. "I did not hear them. Paige said she told the Wind Bird story."

"An old one, but a good one," Whitehorse said. "At least she's sticking to the traditional legends instead of making up her own. I don't know if she knows reality from imagination anymore. She's old."

"No," Juanita quipped. "You're old. She's older."

"There's no need for flattery, now." Whitehorse glared at Juanita. "What else did she tell?"

"Fox and Rabbit," Miguel added. "How Rabbit lost his tail."

"Another good one," Juanita said, waving more customers inside. "Wonder what she'll come up with next week."

"Next week is something about boxes," Miguel added.

Whitehorse stiffened. "What did you say?"

"Just something a little girl said while I was there. That next week Abuela would be telling a story about boxes," Miguel said.

"Nothing strange about that to me," Juanita said. "Remember that time she told the story of the giant watermelon falling from the sky? That was hardly an authentic legend."

"Yes!" Miguel laughed. "And all the seeds fell out when it landed and turned into aliens who only came to earth because there were no tamales on their planet."

"Why so quiet, Whitehorse?" Juanita said. "It's great your sister has a good imagination, keeps her young. Maybe the boxes will have aliens, too – aliens who are coming for nachos this time." She grabbed a hot plate from the pass-through and took it out to a table.

Whitehorse downed his beer and set the empty mug on the bar. He stood up, pulled some folded bills out of his wallet and dropped them on the counter.

"My money by this weekend," Miguel reminded him.

"You'll have it."

It wasn't until Whitehorse climbed into his truck and slammed the door that he let himself explode. Pounding his fist against the steering wheel, he spewed a string of curse words that would make hot sauce sweet in comparison. It was probably just paranoia, he told himself. How could his sister know about the boxes? Hadn't he been cautious when taking telephone calls whenever he was at her place? Had she overheard him on the phone with Hector? Had he let anything slip? No, it had to be coincidence that she had stories about boxes in her head. But coincidence or not, he couldn't take any chances.

CHAPTER EIGHTEEN

Paige hung her robe on the wall hook inside the treatment room and slipped off the gel slippers, setting them on the floor beneath the robe. Slipping under the sheet on the table, she stretched out, face down, and felt her body relax into the heated surface beneath her. A week before, she might have felt too modest to sign up for a massage. But Ana's recommendation of their new therapist had been convincing and, after all, she was in vacation mode.

Being in the spa allowed Paige to still her mind, something she'd never been good at doing. The ambient music spilling from the speakers and the scent of eucalyptus soothed her. And…was that citrus? It smelled like the fresh grated orange zest that her grandmother used to add to cranberry nut bread.

Paige shifted on the table, opening her eyes long enough to admire a trio of candles on a side table, each set at a different height. Closing her eyes again, she adjusted her arms against her side, then above her, elbows out, and then settled with them back by her side.

She heard a light tap, and the door opened and closed gently as the therapist entered. Paige took a deep breath and exhaled, willing her mind to quiet down.

"I'm your massage therapist, Lena. Are you comfortable?" Her soft voice blended with the music.

"Very," Paige said. It was true. The combination of music, candlelight, aromatherapy and heated sheets already had Paige half asleep. Even without a massage, she thought, a nap in a room like this would settle nerves and ease stress.

Lena folded back the portion of sheet that covered Paige's right leg. Paige felt the cooler air settle over her skin, soon followed by the smooth gliding of Lena's hands over her muscles. Scents of sweet almond and rosemary from massage lotion mingled with the eucalyptus and citrus.

"Are we allowed to talk?" Paige whispered.

"Of course, if you want," Lena replied. Paige thought she heard a smile in her voice.

"That feels wonderful," Paige sighed. "This resort is wonderful. Everything here is wonderful."

"As it should be," Lena said, her tone smooth and calm. "Is this the first time you've had a massage?" She applied more lotion and began to work both thumbs into Paige's calf.

"No," Paige said. "But it's been a long time, at least five years. I work a lot and travel a lot. I really don't take vacations."

"Then you're overdue."

"I know," Paige admitted. She could hear the resignation in her own voice.

"I hope you love your work, to spend so much time at it. What do you do, if I may ask?"

"I do love my work," Paige said. "I'm a reporter for *The Manhattan Post*, where I write travel features. Right now I'm working on a series about the Old West."

"And that brought you to Agua Encantada?" Lena let her hands glide downward along Paige's leg and began working on her foot, giving specific pressure points extra attention.

Paige sighed as her muscles continued to loosen. Her feet had always been ticklish, but Lena's touch was purely relaxing.

"Yes. My editor, Susan, and I decided to include the Southwest in the series, and this article on the mineral hot springs will complement a special issue on health. Since I knew I needed a break, I arranged to stay here beyond the time it should take me to finish the assignment."

"You won't regret it," Lena said. "Luz tells me that a lot of her guests return every year the way people have been returning to the waters for centuries." She draped the sheet over Paige's leg and moved around the table to work on her left leg.

Paige relaxed into silence and let herself fall into a half sleep as Lena worked through the muscles of her left leg then her shoulder blades and back. Paige let out a cross between a sigh and a groan. Why had she gone so long without indulging in this treat? She worked hard. She deserved it. She needed to start taking better care of herself. She knew running herself in circles was part of the reason she often felt stressed or had trouble sleeping.

As if she had read Paige's thoughts, Lena said, "Massage therapy is a way to bring body, mind and spirit together, as well as relaxing muscles. We get so scattered these days, we forget to take care of ourselves. This is nothing new. The ancient Chinese and Egyptians knew this; they used massage therapy thousands of years ago."

"That makes sense," Paige managed to mutter as Lena's hands pressed down on her shoulders. Paige followed Lena's directions to roll over onto her back as Lena held the sheet up to give Paige privacy. Once settled again under the sheet, she felt Lena's hands pulling gently on both sides of her neck, stretching the muscles. She could picture her neck growing longer. She felt lighter, even taller. *Must do this more often...*

"Is this what you do full time?" Paige asked. "I hope so, for the sake of your clients and those who haven't discovered you yet."

"No, just part time. I actually gave it up for a while, but I missed helping clients. The spa is one of several reasons I moved to this area a little while ago," Lena answered. "I also work in Luz's store in Tres Palomas. Have you been there?"

"Yes, as a matter of fact," Paige said. "I just visited the other day. She stocks so many wonderful things. I especially love the storyteller dolls. And Ana's jewelry, of course. I bought a pendant and a pair or earrings, the ones with the silver dove design."

"The doves are particularly exquisite. I've bought a few pieces myself."

Paige let her head rest to one side as Lena released it and moved around the table, lifting one of Paige's arms up and tucking the sheet underneath it. Starting with the upper arm, she worked more lotion into the muscles, gently pulling down toward the hands as she went along. After working on Paige's hand, she applied pressure on each of Paige's fingers and then moved to the other arm, repeating the motions.

Maybe I'll just stay on this table for the rest of my visit.

Lena moved once again to Paige's head, this time working along the base of the neck and up around the ears and forehead. She finished with a light scalp massage, finally stepping away.

"I'll be outside when you're ready to come out. Take a few minutes to relax."

It was a solid five minutes before Paige forced herself up off the table. Feeling otherworldly, she donned the spa robe again, and left a generous tip on the counter. When she stepped out into the hall, Lena was waiting to make sure she felt well.

"Thank you so much," Paige said. "That was heavenly. I hope you stick around Tres Palomas. If you do, I'll be tempted to return like all those other believers in the waters and the spa."

"I do love it here, but we'll see. I have obligations that may take me out of town for a few months." Lena said. "Maybe you'll have time for another session before you go back to New York."

"I hope so." Paige thanked Lena again and headed for the dressing room.

CHAPTER NINETEEN

Paige watched as Sylvia, Martha and others mingled in the lobby, surrounded by suitcases. Martha held a foil packet of *pan dulce,* which Luz had wrapped up for her after she'd praised the round, cinnamon and sugar covered buns at breakfast. Several others had taken boxes of food to go, unable to finish the spread Luz had set out for their last morning at the resort.

"Where's your next stop?" Paige asked Sylvia, who was inspecting the glass case that held jewelry, pottery and other artwork.

"Durango, Colorado," Sylvia said, turning to face Paige. She pulled an itinerary out of a tote bag with a Route 66 emblem on the side, unfolding the schedule and looking it over. "Yes, Durango is next, but with some stops along the way. Let's see…."

"I don't need to see the itinerary," Martha piped up. "I studied it yesterday while I soaked in the iron pool. We're stopping at Taos Pueblo and then we go on to visit wool weavers at Tierra Wools before we reach Durango," Martha continued. "Now *that's* what I'm looking forward to, the weavers. I want to pick up some yarn for a sweater I'm planning to make. Maybe purple, if they have it." She beamed. "I love yarn shopping."

"You might need some red, too," Sylvia said.

"Oh, yes, and maybe some pink." Martha tapped a finger against her lips, thinking over the collection of yarn she might acquire.

"We're staying at the Strater Hotel tonight," Sylvia said. "It's supposed to be a 'fine historic hotel.' Apparently, it has antiques in all the guest rooms. Have you heard of it?" she asked Paige.

"It sounds familiar," Paige said. "I've come to love historic hotels. Anything interesting that you'll be seeing in Durango?"

"The railroad," Martha said, her enthusiasm apparent. "It runs between Durango and Silverton. We're riding it tomorrow. Mesa Verde is the next day. From there we go on to Zion and Bryce National Parks."

"It sounds like a wonderful trip, don't you think?" Paige asked Sylvia but realized the woman was still studying the display case. Paige moved closer, looking inside.

Sylvia glanced at Paige and then pointed to a shelf in the case.

"Do you see that pin? The one with the three doves?"

Paige nodded. "It's one of Ana's designs, the girl who works in the spa. That's the pin that looks so much like the one you were wearing the other day."

"Yes, it's just like the one I have," Sylvia said. "But Luz told me yesterday that she's asking almost eighty dollars for it. I'm glad I bought mine where I did, instead of here."

"Did you ever remember where you bought it?"

"Well, I still don't remember exactly," Sylvia said.

Martha, who was sitting nearby, still jotting notes about all the items she planned to knit, paused her writing. "But you found the receipt, Sylvia, remember?"

"Oh," Sylvia said. "Yes, dear, I found the receipt last night when I was packing. It's in my bag somewhere." She rummaged through the Route 66 tote, pulling out a makeup pouch and setting it on the counter. A bag of candy followed, then a deck of cards, an orange scarf with a cactus print, a miniature, plastic kachina doll keychain, and assorted receipts, none of which showed a jewelry purchase.

"Well, I thought I had it," Sylvia sighed as she stuffed her knickknacks back into her bag. "But don't you worry. Just get up there along that stretch of highway, and you'll find all kinds of deals. There's a souvenir stand at every off-ramp. Most carry the same items." She looked around and lowered her voice. "You'll be able to find that exact pin, or something like it. Just don't pay this kind of price for it."

"Thanks, I'll keep that in mind." Paige fought to hide her disappointment. It wasn't Sylvia's fault she hadn't found the receipt. After all, she'd taken the time to dig through her hefty stash.

"The bus is here," Miguel announced, stepping into the lobby. Indeed, the large tour bus that had dropped them off days before had pulled up in front. A shuffling of feet followed the announcement. Miguel grabbed two suitcases, heading back to the bus to load them into the compartment beneath the passenger section. Paige watched as he returned and retrieved two more, then two after that. By the time the tour group had boarded the bus, he had finished loading the bags. The bus driver pulled the compartment cover down and secured it, patted the side of the vehicle and entered the bus. He did a quick head count and roll call, checking off names on a clipboard. Satisfied everyone was on board, he climbed into the driver's seat.

Paige leaned against the doorway of the resort office, watching the group members squirm around in their seats, getting comfortable. She noticed Sylvia waving at her, and she waved back. This just made Sylvia wave more frantically, and Paige realized she wasn't just saying goodbye, Sylvia was calling her over. Paige stepped up to the bus's window, trying not to breathe the exhaust fumes surrounding the bus. Sylvia cracked the window open the few inches the safety bar allowed.

"Here's that receipt," Sylvia said, shoving a small paper through the opening. "It was in my pocket. I found it when I put the jacket up above the seat."

Paige took the paper as the bus driver stepped on the gas and began to move forward.

"Now, you get yourself one of those pretty pins," Sylvia called out, cupping her mouth and then waving again as the bus pulled away.

"I'll try!" Paige shouted back. *You'd better believe I'll try.*

CHAPTER TWENTY

Paige watched Luz clear the breakfast plates off the tables. Remnants of the meal were non-existent, as guests had devoured every last morsel of the tomato, cheddar cheese and cilantro frittata. Only a basket of jalapeño corn muffins remained. Paige pushed it to the side, to avoid temptation. What was it about the southwestern food that made her want to take "just one more bite?" Maybe the spices were the lure. The food she'd encountered since arriving in Tres Palomas was perfect comfort food with a twist.

Standing up, Paige gathered her notebook and pen, taking one more sip of coffee before pushing her chair in. Since the tour group had left, the notebook had been a good companion. The few other guests had already finished their meals and headed out before Paige arrived for breakfast. Conveniently, she'd had a table to herself, with plenty of time to jot down thoughts between bites. She'd rearranged her article outline to incorporate more aspects of the local way of life, making a list of specifics to double-check. Like the origin of some of Abuela's stories. This reminded her that it was Sunday, and she had only a half hour to get to St. Bernadette's to hear Abuela's weekly performance.

This also meant she only had three more days to finish the article and enjoy what she could of vacation time before returning to New York. Paige sighed at this thought. Not only was she unprepared to go back to the city, but she felt uneasy. Maybe it was because of the tense phone conversation she'd had with Jake. Maybe it was because the other two trips had been amazing and romantic *because* Jake was involved, and she missed that involvement. She knew this assignment would be different if for no other reason than the distance between New Mexico and Wyoming. She hadn't expected to see Jake. But she also hadn't expected the trip to cause a conflict. Now that the tour group was gone, she had more time to think about the situation with Jake. Had they argued? It had been close. At least she'd had the good sense to end the call before the discussion escalated. Still, jealousy? All because she mentioned a man she'd met only a few times? It was silly, childish even.

Paige thought this over as she walked back to the casita. This was one stage of a relationship that she'd never liked, when both sides were weighing the possibility of a future, yet neither wanted to be the first to say this out loud. In the past, this was when she'd often been the one to turn away. And the current confusion about her relationship with Jake was a perfect example why. They'd reached a point where they either needed to move forward or back away. Standing still wasn't an option. Moving forward was scary, but so was stepping back. One way or another, something would have to happen.

Back in the casita, Paige closed the door and set her notebook and pen on the desk. She sat on the bed, picked up her cell phone from the nightstand and looked at it. Calling Jake would be easy, just fingertips touching numbers. But she'd gone two days without calling and also hadn't heard from him. No, she wasn't going to make the first move. Besides, she needed to hurry if she wanted to hear Abuela's stories that morning. She'd be gone by the following Sunday, so this was her last chance. She gathered her things, glanced quickly at her reflection – tousled hair, old sweatshirt, but nothing that would cause alarm – and left for town.

Parked cars lined both sides of the street in front of St. Bernadette's, overflow from the small dirt parking lot on one side of the church. Those worshipers who weren't planning to remain after Mass to hear Abuela's stories were already loading their families in cars. Paige realized her timing was perfect as she filled the first freed parking spot. Taking only keys with her, she locked the car and walked toward the church.

Small groups stood gathered in the courtyard, just as they had the week before. Some carried on conversations, while others simply waited. The young boy and girl she'd noticed the previous Sunday played in front of the fountain. Paige smiled. Hopefully the young girl would get the story about boxes that she'd requested. Or, better yet, she'd have forgotten about the whole box-fox confusion and would just enjoy whatever stories the old woman had to tell.

Paige stepped through the gate to the church courtyard and looked around, sensing the crowd was impatient. Or was it uneasy? She scanned the faces of those nearest her, which reinforced her appraisal. The townsfolk looked concerned. Even Father John, who'd finished his post-service handshakes on the church steps, was watching the crowd with a frown. Two women approached him, and he listened intently as he leaned forward. His expression looked reassuring as he spoke to them, but Paige was certain she saw a trace of worry on his face. She crossed the courtyard and climbed the few stairs to reach him.

"Good morning, Father John," Paige said, reintroducing herself to the parish priest. "I came to hear the storyteller again."

The priest shook her hand, but glanced over her head before speaking, preoccupied with the crowd.

"What's going on?" Paige followed the direction of his gaze, seeing the same crowd she'd just passed through, groups of people conversing, children playing and…an empty cement bench surrounding the fountain. "Oh," she said. "Abuela isn't here today?" She hesitated as she spoke, realizing the absence of an elderly person could mean bad news.

"No," the priest said, lines of worry now obvious on his face. "She didn't show up today. She always attends Mass and then moves outside to tell her stories. But she wasn't here at all today, not even for the service."

"Has she ever missed before?" Paige asked

"Never."

"*Padre Juan*," one woman called, rounding the side of the church and climbing the steps. A second woman followed just behind. Lace scarves covered the heads of both women, who appeared to be in their seventies.

"*No esta*," the first woman said, slightly out of breath.

"She is not there," the second added, shaking her head.

Father John turned to Paige to explain, "Abuela lives behind the church. Consuela and Alma are from our women's group and went to see if Abuela might be ill and resting, but she isn't there."

"Could I see her room?" As soon as she asked, Paige realized it might seem an odd question from a stranger, but she hoped her meeting with the priest last week might be enough for him to agree. It was.

"Yes, I don't see why not," he said. "Maybe the eyes of a visitor will see something we don't." He motioned for

Consuela and Alma to lead the way, staying by the church to speak with other parishioners who were approaching him.

Paige followed as the women scurried alongside the church. Their eagerness hinted of a hope that they might have missed Abuela the first time, a thought that Paige shared. Maybe the storyteller had stepped out briefly, had done something as simple as going for a short walk and forgetting the time.

The small room was remarkably bare. A twin bed rested against one wall, a metal crucifix hanging above it. A table with two chairs sat on a braided rug. Other furniture included a chest of drawers, a smaller table that served as a nightstand, and a compact refrigerator. A mirror hung over the dresser with a string of rosary beads dangling from it. Two colored paper flowers in a pottery vase were a bright contrast to the otherwise dull surroundings. Abuela was not there.

Paige walked to a closet on the far side of the room and opened the doors. She sensed the women disapproved; probably they felt she was invading the storyteller's privacy. But she wasn't there to snoop. She was hoping to find some sign of where Abuela might be.

She tried to reassure them of her motives. "I don't mean to pry, but I'm a reporter, and sometimes I see things others miss." Paige pulled a hanger with a brown coat out and held it up. "Is this the jacket she usually wears?"

"No," both women said at once.

"Show me which jacket she usually wears," Paige said, gesturing toward the closet. The women looked at each other, hesitating. "Ladies, please. You might be able to help find her."

After Consuela looked at the closet rack, she said, "The jacket she likes to wear is not here."

"That means she probably has it with her," Paige said. She studied the closet more closely. "There are very few clothes here," she added.

"Abuela doesn't own much," Alma said. "She gives away anything that is given to her, always saying someone else needs it more than she does. But…" The woman paused, stepping closer to the closet. "She does have more than this. A few blouses are missing."

"Her favorite skirt, too," the first woman said. "It is long, made from a woven fabric."

"So, several articles of clothing are missing?" Paige glanced from one face to the other; the women nodded. She walked back to the front door, inspecting the lock. "No one seems to have tampered with the lock, and closet doors and dresser drawers were closed when we came in. The bed is made."

The women stared at Paige, puzzled.

"What I'm trying to say is that I think your storyteller, Abuela, went on a trip."

"A trip?" The women exchanged glances. "She does not go on trips. Her life is here. She would not go anywhere."

The other woman gasped. "She has been kidnapped!"

"What? Kidnapped?" Father John's worried voice echoed from the doorway.

"No," Paige said. "I don't think so. Nothing has been disturbed or broken. She knew she was going somewhere. No one forced her to go. Does she have a car?"

"No," Father John said. "She never learned to drive. She has no use for a car. If she needs to get groceries or anything else, someone always volunteers to drive her."

Paige looked around the room again. "There's no note anywhere."

"I don't think she ever learned to read or write, either," the priest said.

"So she knew she was going somewhere and took some clothes. Someone would have had to drive her. There hasn't been a struggle here, which means she must have gone with someone she knows." Paige paused. "So who would that be?"

"The only one I can think of is her brother, Charlie Whitehorse," Father John said. "I can't imagine why he'd take her anywhere."

"Abuela and Whitehorse are related?" Paige could hardly believe two such different people were brother and sister. Conflicting thoughts ran through her mind as she headed to the door. "I have to go find someone."

"Whitehorse?" one of the women asked.

"No," Paige said. "I need to find Miguel."

"Well, you won't find him here." Father John almost smiled. Despite the seriousness of the situation, Paige fought back a laugh.

"No, but I think I know where he is. And if we can find Miguel, we can find Whitehorse. And I think if we find Whitehorse, we'll find Abuela."

To the confusion of the women and the priest, Paige left them standing in the room and made a beeline for her car.

CHAPTER TWENTY-ONE

The parking lot at the Coyote Cantina was empty, except for a couple of trucks parked near the front. Whitehorse's truck was missing, but Miguel's was there, as Paige had hoped it would be. She parked next to it and hurried inside. Two customers Paige didn't know occupied a corner table. A half-empty beer glass sat on the bar counter in front of an empty chair. Otherwise, the watering hole was empty.

Juanita looked up from wiping down the bar. "What can I get you? Beer? Coffee?"

"Actually, I'm looking for Miguel," Paige said. "His truck's out front, so he must be here."

Juanita laughed. "Oh, no, don't tell me he's got his hooks into you already."

"I need to talk to him," Paige said, ignoring the comment. If she hadn't been worried about Abuela, she might have laughed back. "It's important. Abuela's gone missing and I think he can help find her."

"Abuela's missing?" Juanita turned serious. "Wasn't she in the church courtyard this morning? That doesn't make sense. She never goes anywhere."

"Yes, that's exactly what everyone has been saying," Paige said, still scanning the room for Miguel. "And no, she didn't show up this morning. She wasn't in her room and some of her clothes are missing."

"Whose clothes are missing?"

Paige turned to see Miguel emerging from the restroom. "I like the sound of that, depending on who it is, of course." Miguel's smirk annoyed Paige, but she didn't have time to worry about an attitude adjustment.

"Abuela's," Paige said.

Miguel looked confused. "Abuela's clothes are missing?"

"*ABUELA* is missing, you moron," Juanita said. She grabbed the beer glass off the counter and dumped its contents in the sink. "Forget the beer. See if you can help find her."

"Father John thinks she might be with Whitehorse," Paige said, "and you're probably the only one who knows where he is."

"I have no idea where Whitehorse is. Juanita, have you seen him today?" Miguel was starting to look upset.

"No, he hasn't been in. Not yesterday either, now that I think of it." Juanita set the bar towel down and frowned. "And it's not like him to skip a day, especially a Saturday. Not unless he goes out of town to gamble."

"We just have to find him," Paige said. "Hopefully Abuela is with him. If not, he needs to know she's missing."

"I thought he stopped the gambling," Miguel said.

"No, Miguel. You know I overhear a lot of things around this place and I usually keep my mouth shut." Juanita leaned forward and lowered her voice so the customers at the back table wouldn't hear. "But since it sounds like Abuela might be in trouble, I'd better tell you: I think Whitehorse has been back at it again."

"Why do you say that?" Miguel asked.

"Phone calls," Juanita said. "He gets phone calls in here sometimes that make him spit out some mighty harsh words. And he looks angry and scared when he gets off the phone. Only time I've ever seen that look on him is when he's on a gambling binge. And I don't like the sound of that guy's voice who calls him, either. Business-like but gruff. I'm telling you, it's no friend of his. Mind you, you didn't hear any of this from me. But if it helps you find Abuela, take it and run."

Miguel grabbed his keys off the bar, motioning to Paige. "Follow me back to the resort." He called back to Juanita as he disappeared through the front door, "I owe you for that beer."

"For once I don't care," Juanita said. "Just get out there and find Whitehorse and his sister."

Paige gripped the steering wheel of her rental car tightly as she followed Miguel back to Agua Encantada. Between the dust blowing upward from behind his truck's wheels and the speed he was driving, she could barely keep up. She was relieved when they both pulled up in front of the resort office. She turned the ignition off, took a deep breath and climbed out of the car. Miguel was already inside the office talking to Marisol when Paige came through the door.

"Why would I know where Whitehorse is, Miguel?" Marisol looked even more confused than the crowd at the church. "He's *your* drinking buddy. You're the one who should know how to keep tabs on him, if anyone should. Did you try looking at the Coyote?"

"He is not my drinking buddy, or any kind of buddy of mine," Miguel said. "And, yes, I tried the Coyote and he was not there. Juanita has not seen him, either. I just wondered if you had seen him." Miguel threw a concerned look at Paige and then looked back at Marisol. "Never mind, just take care

131

of Josie and Rico. Make sure to feed them. And tell Ana I am going out of town, so she will not worry."

"Oh, Ana didn't come in today," Marisol said. "I thought you knew. Lena called to say she opened the spa for her, said Ana wasn't feeling well."

"What?" Miguel said. "Ana is never sick. Did you try calling her house?"

Marisol frowned. "No, I didn't think to. The spa's only been open a couple hours and Lena just called up here twenty minutes ago to tell me she was covering for the day."

"Didn't you have to give her a key to get in?" Paige asked.

"No, I assume she got the key from Ana."

"Ana would not loan out her key to the spa," Miguel said. "Not even to Lena. You have keys, right?"

"Sure, we have keys to everywhere on the property," Marisol said, reaching below the counter and pulling out a cluster of keys on a wide metal loop. "For maintenance issues, or any sort of emergency when you're not around." She sorted through the keys, flipping each one over as she moved on to the next. As she reached the end of the set, she frowned. "I don't see the spa key, though. And no one asked to borrow it. Maybe Lena took it while I was doing the breakfast dishes?"

"That's odd she wouldn't have told you," Paige said. "Maybe someone else took the key?" She tried to keep her voice even, to avoid upsetting Miguel, but it was too late. He was already out the door, Paige right behind him. Reaching the spa, they came to an abrupt halt. The door was locked.

"Lena?" Miguel shook the door handle, which refused to budge. He knocked on the door, his shouts growing louder. "Lena, open up!" He reached in his pocket for keys, coming up empty. Again he grabbed the door handle and tried to yank it open.

"My keys are in the truck." Miguel turned to start for the parking lot.

"No, follow me," Paige said, tugging on his shirt. "We can go around the back."

Miguel followed Paige around to the side fence and watched as she scaled it and dropped down on the other side. He did the same, scrambling after her as she reached the back window.

"Do I even want to know how you know this?" Miguel's breathing was ragged.

"Probably not, but it doesn't matter right now, does it?"

"Absolutely not."

"Then grab that window and shake the frame," Paige said. "I'm not tall enough to reach it, but you should be able to. The inside latch is loose. You can pull it open."

Miguel stretched up to the window and rattled the frame, but the window stayed closed. Paige glanced around on the ground and picked up a small stick. "Try this."

"I have a better idea," Miguel said, reaching into his pocket and pulling out a pocketknife. Prying it open, he wedged the blade between the window and the frame, maneuvering the space until the window popped open.

Again, Miguel called out, "Lena?" No answer.

"Now what?" Miguel said, looking at Paige. "I cannot fit through that window."

"But I can," Paige said, threading her fingers together to demonstrate a step. Miguel understood and laced his fingers into a step, catching Paige's foot and boosting her up high enough to climb through the window. She grasped the upper edge of the window frame and maneuvered her legs in first.

"Go back around to the front door," Paige shouted as she dropped inside the building.

Despite the aroma of eucalyptus, the adrenaline running through Paige's system nullified spa's usual serenity. The absence of music was also eerie, the silence intensifying the sense of menace.

Paige started through the dark building, grateful for the light from the adobe structure's few windows. Calling out for Lena, she made her way to the front door and unlocked it, stepping back quickly as Miguel rushed in.

"Did you find Lena?" Miguel said.

"I called her name, but didn't get an answer. Check the treatment rooms down the hall. I'll look in the dressing room." Paige pointed Miguel in one direction and headed in the other.

"Lena?" Paige called, opening the door to the dressing room. She patted the wall, found the light switch and turned it on, but the room was empty. A quick check of the restroom had the same result.

"Paige, down here," Miguel shouted. "Hurry!"

Sprinting, Paige followed Miguel's shouts to the treatment room where she'd had the massage just days before. But, to her shock, it was not Lena she saw. Instead, Ana huddled on the floor in the corner of the room, wrists and ankles tied together. Miguel was working frantically to loosen a thick cloth tied around her mouth. When he finished, Ana sputtered thanks and fought to catch her breath.

"Ana," Miguel cried, starting in on the rope around her wrists. "Lena did this to you? Why? Why would she?"

Ana pulled back. "No, of course Lena did not do this...why would you even think that?"

"She called Marisol and told her you were sick and that she was working for you today," Paige said.

"That doesn't make sense. Lena wasn't even here this morning. I opened the spa, just like I always do on Sundays. But...." Ana's eyes filled with fear.

"Then who did this to you?" Miguel shouted.

"A man came in...." Ana managed, rubbing the rope marks on her wrists as Miguel untied the ones around her ankles.

"Whitehorse?" Paige asked. She grabbed a box of tissues from the counter and offered it to Ana, who pulled two sheets from the container as tears rolled down her face.

"No, not Whitehorse," Ana said, dabbing her eyes with the tissues. "I don't know who the man was. I'd never seen him before."

"Did he hurt you?" Miguel shouted. "Because if he did...."

"No, Miguel, no!" Ana cried. "Please do not go crazy. He did not hurt me!"

Paige left the room and returned quickly. "I called the office and asked Marisol to call the police. They'll want a description. Can you remember what the man looked like?"

"I do not know. I was scared. It happened so quickly. I do remember he was tall and heavy and had a deep voice. I thought...." Ana started shaking again. Miguel cursed and left the room.

"Miguel, wait," Ana called.

"It'll be OK," Paige said, her voice soothing, but sympathetic. "Just tell the police whatever you remember when they get here."

"Please, go follow my brother," Ana pleaded. "He does not think clearly when upset. He is going to do something stupid, I just know it."

Paige glanced over her shoulder, hoping Miguel would return but her intuition told her Ana was right; he was headed for trouble.

"Come with me, then," Paige said. "I'm not leaving you here alone. I'll walk you over to the office so you can stay with Marisol. Then I'll go find Miguel, I promise."

Paige helped Ana to her feet and led her out of the spa building and across the property to the office, where Marisol took over. With Ana safely in Marisol's hands, Paige took off after Miguel. It didn't take long to locate him; she just followed the cursing and door slamming coming from the direction of his truck.

"Miguel, what are you doing?" Paige hurried to the truck, catching him just as he was climbing into the driver's seat.

"What do you think I am doing?" he snapped. "I'm going to find the guy who did this to Ana."

"Then I'm going with you," Paige said, rounding the front of the truck. She climbed into the passenger seat, despite protests from Miguel. "You're too upset to drive anywhere alone. Besides, I told your sister I'd follow you.

"No," Miguel insisted. "She should not be left alone now."

Paige refused to move. "Marisol is with her, and the police are on their way. She'll be all right. I'm going with you. I promised Ana."

"You are one stubborn woman, you know?"

"So I've been told."

Miguel backed the truck away from the office and took off. To Paige's confusion, he didn't head straight for the resort driveway, but pulled up in front of Paige's casita."

"No," Paige said, crossing her arms. "I'm not getting out. I'm going with you."

"Fine. Then grab a toothbrush and a change of clothes."

"What? Why?"

"Because I know where we need to look and it is not in Tres Palomas." Miguel's words rushed out. "Or you can be smart and stay here."

"No," Paige repeated, jumping out. "Just wait. And don't think about taking off, either. I'll just follow you in my car." She ran into the casita and tossed a change of clothes and toothbrush in her overnight bag, pausing for only a second. *This won't be easy to explain to Jake.* Making sure she had her cell phone in her pocket, she rushed back to the truck.

Miguel stepped on the gas the second she closed the door and took off up the driveway, passing the incoming police car on the way out. He lifted a hand in greeting, but didn't stop.

"So where are we going?" Paige struggled against the movement of the vehicle to put her seatbelt on.

"To find Whitehorse."

CHAPTER TWENTY-TWO

Whitehorse opened the door to the storage shed and stepped inside, a plate of *carne asada* in one hand, a bottle of water in the other. He looked at the makeshift sitting area his sister had made from Navajo blankets and an old wooden cot, and felt a stab of guilt.

"You shouldn't be out here, *hermana*. I told you I would get food and bring it back to you. I told you to stay in the trailer." Hector never bothered with the trailer. It was the safest place for Abuela to be.

"The door was open," Abuela said. "You took a long time. I decided to walk while I waited for you."

"She's fine, Whitehorse." The voice came from the worktable. "Though you didn't do her any favors by bringing her to Gallup."

"And what are *you* doing here, Lena?" Whitehorse barked.

"I'm here to protect my investment."

"*Your* investment?"

"Yes, *my* investment," Lena said. "And Hector's, of course."

If Whitehorse hadn't been so distraught over the mess he'd gotten his sister into he would have laughed. "You've been in on this all along? Don't fool yourself. Hector's using you, just like he uses everyone."

"You're wrong," Lena snapped. "Besides, you're one to talk, Whitehorse. You're in a lot deeper with Hector than I am. At least I don't owe him money."

Whitehorse exploded. "I *wouldn't* owe him money now if not for the two of you scheming! This whole enterprise was supposed to get me out of debt, not dig the hole deeper."

"You can't blame your problems on anyone but yourself, Whitehorse. You've been gambling longer than I've been alive and you know the consequences, so don't blame me."

Lena crossed the storage unit and pulled a carton from the top of a stack of boxes. Bringing it to the worktable, she dropped it forcibly and used a box cutter to slice the top open. Reaching in, she pulled out large plastic bags and set them on the table. Grabbing a clipboard with paperwork and a pen, she focused on the task at hand.

Whitehorse looked at Abuela, who simply shook her head, resigned.

"Why did you bring her out here, anyway," Lena said, nodding toward Abuela as she studied the plastic bags and checked off items. She set the clipboard down. "I expected to be alone this morning. Imagine my surprise when Abuela wandered in. And not a pleasant surprise, either. This just makes one more person who has to keep quiet."

"I was worried she'd overheard something she shouldn't have," Whitehorse said. "Miguel said she was going to tell a story about boxes this week." He turned to his sister. "Is that right?"

"Yes," Abuela said. "A young girl asked for a story about boxes."

"And what story were you going to tell, Abuela?" Lena asked.

"Boxes represent what we do not know. We cannot see in from outside." Abuela made the shape of a box with her fingers.

"So what is in the boxes, Abuela?" Lena asked, pushing forward.

"Anything," Abuela said. "Or nothing. That is the point of the story. It is the unknown that we question, that is what is in the boxes."

"You see?" Lena said, turning back to Whitehorse. "Now look what you've done. Your sister has no idea what's in *these* boxes. You should have left well enough alone. What do you think happened when people didn't see her after Mass today?"

Whitehorse began to pace. "I wasn't thinking about that. I just didn't want her telling anyone about the boxes."

"You weren't thinking at all," Lena snapped. "Now they'll be looking for her, all of them: Father John, the kids who stay after Mass to hear her every week, Luz, Marisol, Miguel, that nosy reporter who's staying at the resort.... And everyone's first thought will be that she's with you."

"No one in Tres Palomas knows where this place is," Whitehorse said. "They don't even know I have property out here. They all figure I go out of town to gamble, which is true."

"Yes, but it's not the whole truth. And with your sister missing, this little side business is at risk."

"First of all," Whitehorse spit out, "this isn't *my* little side business. Hector built this storage unit and that dinky trading post out on the highway. All I had was a quiet trailer. The rest of it is all his." At the mention of Hector, Abuela glanced at Whitehorse, eyebrows rising.

"And mine," Lena added as she dumped the contents of one bag on the table. A batch of smaller plastic bags spread out across the surface filled with silver pins, earrings and pendants.

"Fine, delude yourself," Whitehorse said. "And, second of all, my sister isn't missing, she's just visiting. I panicked about the box story and brought her out here, but obviously I was wrong. Look, I'll show you." Turning to his sister, he asked, "What's in the boxes, *hermana*?"

"As I said, no one knows what is in boxes," Abuela said.

"No, *hermana*," Whitehorse insisted. "What's in *these* boxes, here in the storage shed?"

Abuela frowned, looking across the shed at Lena and the table, and then turning back to Whitehorse.

"Do you think I'm blind, *hermano*? Plastic bags. These boxes are full of plastic bags. You can see that as well as I can."

"And what's in the plastic bags, Abuela?" Lena asked.

"I do not know. Glittery things. Secrets," Abuela said.

"You see?" Whitehorse faced Lena and stretched both arms out to the side. "We'll drive back to Tres Palomas tomorrow. No one will think anything."

"I don't think so." A deep voice startled all three of them.

Turning toward the doorway, Whitehorse lashed out verbally at the tall silhouette that filled the frame.

"What do you mean you 'don't think so,' Hector," Whitehorse said. "My sister has nothing to do with any of this."

"You should have thought about that before you brought her out here," Hector said. "I don't invest this much into anything without protecting my interests." He faced Lena. "Did you sort those shipments to go out to the other trading posts?"

"Yes," Lena said, flipping through a few sheets on her clipboard. "Everything is ready: three shipments to go up north to Shiprock, Farmington and Tucumcari, plus four down to Lordsburg, Deming, Mesilla and Santa Teresa." She set the paperwork down and looked up at Hector. "You know, you should really let me do the packing and shipping myself, instead of having those two creepy assistants of yours do it. It's all ready to go once I finish the inventory and divide it between trading posts. You should give me the key to the closet of shipping supplies." Lena gestured to a small door in a back corner, confident and bossy. "And we should use UPS. Your delivery guys spend a lot on gas, not to mention using cash for that. You could at least give them a credit card."

"I thought we were only selling these pieces here," Whitehorse said. "Is this why you have all this stock?" He took a step toward Hector, but stopped as the bookie pulled a knife out of his belt.

"We're done, Whitehorse," Hector said calmly. "You've been a waste of my time from the start. I should have put an end to this as soon as I got my hands on your property."

"You've made plenty of money off me," Whitehorse pointed out.

Hector laughed. "A drop in the bucket, trust me. Nothing worth the headache of dealing with you. I could have set up this operation anywhere."

"That's right, Hector," Lena said, leaving the table and approaching him with a smile. "We need to think about moving forward. We don't need Whitehorse anymore. Or his sister. Or...." She froze as Hector faced her, knife still in hand. "Or," she repeated, confused.

"Or you, Lena," Hector said. "You're as stupid as the rest of them."

"But...but I helped you...you said...we were going to...."

"Like I said, you're as stupid as the rest of them." He motioned with the knife for Lena to move over to join Whitehorse and Abuela.

"What are you doing, Hector?" Lena asked, joining the others. "Our whole inventory is in here. Everything we worked for."

"Trust me, you have no idea what's here," Hector said. "And there's no 'our' in this venture, or haven't you figured that out yet? It's enough I had to pay for the samples Whitehorse picked up from you at that store."

"And now, with the extra stash of jewelry from the spa building, I've got just what I wanted," Hector said. "Never limit your sources."

"What stash in the spa building?" Whitehorse asked.

"Nothing you need to worry about." Hector pulled a roll of cording off a hook on the wall. Keeping an eye on the trio, he cut off pieces and tossed them to Whitehorse.

"Tie them up," he said. "Hands and feet." At Whitehorse's shocked expression, he repeated the order. "Now, Whitehorse, both of them."

"Let me take my sister home. She has nothing to do with this."

"She does now. She's here. Tie her up. Lena, too. And make it quick. You're coming with me."

Hector blew across the tip of his knife blade and pointed it back at the group, waiting while Whitehorse followed his orders. Abuela sat stoic and silent during the ordeal. Lena, however, screamed obscenities. Once satisfied the women couldn't get away, Hector shoved Whitehorse out the door, padlocked it and pocketed the key.

CHAPTER TWENTY-THREE

Paige struggled to dial Jake's number as the bouncing of Miguel's truck interfered with the dexterity of her fingers. She'd called twice already, once just after leaving Agua Encantada and again as they caught I-25 south from Santa Fe. Both times she'd reached voice mail, which made her resent Jake's dismissive view of cell phones. It was just another reason a long distance relationship with him was frustrating. With modern technology, it should be easier to reach him. Instead, they continued a pattern of missed messages and miscommunication.

Hearing the number ringing, Paige felt hopeful she'd get through this time. Those hopes were dashed when the connection cut out. Looking at her phone, she cursed and dropped it into her lap.

"No answer again?" Miguel asked, swerving to avoid rolling tumbleweed, then straightening back out.

"No service," Paige said, looking out the truck's passenger window. The sun was getting lower on the horizon. It was almost evening and she still hadn't reached him. And now, if he returned one of her messages, he wouldn't be able to reach her, either. *Why is it always like this? The distance, the difficulty reaching each other?*

"You did not have to come along, you know," Miguel said. "I tried to tell you not to. You are too stubborn for your own good." He leaned forward and switched on the radio, turning the dial to adjust the static. Paige only half-listened, absorbing little of what Miguel was saying and understanding none of what came out of the radio. *La Jefa 105.1 FM cuenta con la mejor música regional mexicana del momento...*

Paige glanced at her cell phone again. *Still no service.* Resigned, she slid the cell phone into her pocket and looked back out the window, slumping down in her seat. "Where are we, anyway? We've been driving for hours."

"West of Albuquerque, east of Gallup," Miguel said.

"Gallup," Paige repeated. She rummaged through her overnight bag and pulled out a slip of paper. "That's the town on this receipt, where Sylvia bought the pin with Ana's design."

"Is there an address?"

"No, just the amount paid and name of the town," Paige said.

"We can look for it after we find Whitehorse. He will know who did this to Ana. If not, his gambling buddies will. I know where to track him down."

"His gambling buddies?"

"Whitehorse has always had a gambling problem," Miguel said. "He can usually get himself out of trouble, but I think he is in too deep this time, way too deep. Somehow that is connected to Abuela going missing."

"But why would that have anything to do with your sister?" Paige looked at Miguel. "Are these people trying to scare you by threatening to hurt Ana?"

"No," Miguel said. "I think Ana just happened to be at the spa at the wrong time. This is not about me. It is about Whitehorse and his gambling."

Paige sat up straighter, trying to put the pieces together. "I'm still not getting the connection. Why would these people even be in the spa? And are you involved with the gambling, too?"

Miguel shook his head, ignoring the first question. "No. I went up to Whitehorse's favorite casino with him a few times, but I stopped going about a year ago. Whitehorse does not have good judgment when it comes to the people he works with."

Paige pulled her cell phone out of her pocket and glanced at it. *Still no service.*

"No phone calls from anyone special?" Miguel smiled as he pulled off the interstate and onto a frontage road. Paige chose not to respond. A conversation with Miguel about Jake wouldn't be productive. She geared the discussion back to the current situation.

"I take it Whitehorse's bookie is not a nice guy."

"Bookies in general are not nice guys, but this one?" Miguel shook his head. "I have never met him, but I have heard stories."

"Like what?"

"Nothing you want to hear, trust me."

Paige turned and looked out the window again. The sun was almost down. She was out in the middle of New Mexico, without cell service, in a truck with a man she'd only known for a week. She stole a quick glance at Miguel. *What was I thinking?*

"Where are we going, anyway?"

A flashy neon sign appeared ahead, growing larger as they approached it. Miguel answered Paige's question by turning into the lot, pulling into a parking spot and setting the emergency brake. Paige looked out at the expansive building and up at the sign.

"Tierra Roja Casino?"

"Good that you can read, even if you do not know how to roll a double 'r' correctly."

Paige smacked Miguel's shoulder. Without looking at him, she knew he was smiling.

"Don't make fun of my Spanish," Paige quipped.

"I would never, *Sonrisa*."

"And stop the '*Sonrisa*' stuff, Miguel. It's flattering, but you know I'm not available."

"Are you sure about that?"

Miguel didn't wait for an answer, but let the engine idle as he got out of the truck and looked around the parking lot. He circled the truck, arriving at Paige's door as she was opening it. Pushing it closed, he tapped on the window.

"Now what?" she said, reluctantly rolling the window down. "You don't think I came all this way to sit in your truck, do you?" She yanked on the door handle, but Miguel pressed against the door, his face a few inches from Paige's as he leaned in the open window. A nervous flutter ran through Paige's body. *But he is not Jake....*

"Whitehorse's truck is not here. But I want to check the casino out," Miguel whispered. "See if his bookie is here, or if anyone in the casino has seen him. Promise me you will stay in the truck."

"Maybe," Paige said. She had no intention of being left behind.

"I mean it, Paige. Stay here." Miguel's voice was firm. "Let me make sure it is safe. If Whitehorse's bookie is here, you should stay in the truck. I will check. Then you can come in."

"Fine, I'll wait," Paige lied. She watched Miguel sprint toward the casino. As soon as he disappeared inside, she turned off the ignition and got out of the truck. Glancing quickly in both directions, she hurried across the parking lot and into the building.

CHAPTER TWENTY-FOUR

As she stepped inside Tierra Roja Casino, Paige blinked at the bright lights, then coughed, the thick smoke that hovered across the room assaulting her. She'd never been comfortable around smoke, even outdoors. But inside the building, it felt suffocating. Apparently gambling and nicotine addictions went hand in hand. In addition, the low hum of voices and sharp ping of slot machines added to the claustrophobic atmosphere.

She glanced around, but saw no sign of Miguel. Pulling out her cell phone, her heart leapt at the sight of cell service. It crashed just as quickly when a call to Jake went to voice mail. Two messages from him did nothing to calm her down. He said the first time, "Call me," and the second, "Where are you?" Did he think she was avoiding his calls? She left a quick voice mail and put the phone away.

A cocktail waitress wearing satin shorts and a low-cut tank top offered Paige a drink. Paige shook her head and mumbled that she was just looking for someone. The server moved on to a table to take orders from a group of men hunched over a game of cards. Blackjack? Poker? Paige had no idea and didn't care. Her only goal now was finding Miguel, who seemed to have disappeared.

Paige circled the room, intrigued by the activity, by the serious focus on some faces and carefree expressions of others. Clearly some of the patrons took their gambling seriously, while others were just there to have fun. And some were there to get into trouble, whether intentionally or not. It had sounded, from Miguel's comments, like Whitehorse fell into the latter category. Considering what had happened to Ana, as well as the missing status of Abuela, Paige was sure of it. The question was what connected the events. Hopefully, the casino held the key.

"Are you looking for someone?"

Paige turned toward the casually, yet impeccably, dressed man who now stood beside her. He was dignified, measured and controlled, with a neat haircut and perfect manicure.

"Yes," she stuttered, unnerved at the unexpected question. "A man about your height with long hair pulled back into a ponytail."

"Ah, in his thirties, maybe? Handsome? Wearing jeans and a button-down shirt of some sort?"

"Yes," Paige answered, reluctant to agree to the handsome comment, though there was no question it was true.

When the man steepled his fingers, his shirt sleeve rose to reveal a watch that promptly reflected the casino lights. Paige was hardly an expert on jewelry, but his watch looked expensive, as did his diamond cufflinks. *Were those real?*

"I believe the person you're looking for went into a back room over there." The man indicated the far side of the casino. "If you'd like, I can take you back."

"No, that's OK," Paige said. Even with her penchant for letting curiosity control her, she was too smart to go into a back room with a man she didn't know. The casino itself felt ominous enough. *But it wouldn't hurt to ask questions, would it?*

"Maybe you can help, though. He – the man I was asking about – and I are looking for a man named Charlie Whitehorse. Have you seen him?"

Paige caught the man's brief frown before he smoothed his expression into nonchalance.

"Charlie Whitehorse? No, I can't say I've seen him recently." The man glanced around the casino, a gesture Paige was certain to be an act. Whether Whitehorse was there or not, he wasn't about to say. At a loss, Paige excused herself and moved away, making a conscious effort not to look back. She could sense the man's eyes following her. Which was why she jumped when she felt a firm hand grab her arm.

"What are you doing in here?"

Paige turned to find herself face to face with Miguel.

"I told you to stay out until I made sure it was safe." Miguel let go of Paige's arm and massaged the back of his neck, looking around.

"So, is it? Safe, that is?" Paige rubbed her arm, which smarted from Miguel's grasp.

"Well, Whitehorse is not here, as far as I can tell," Miguel said. "And no one has seen Hector or any of his thugs."

"I thought we were looking for Whitehorse." Paige sighed, exasperated. "Would you please tell me what's going on? And wait...what thugs?"

"You should not even be here. I should have thrown you out of the truck when you first got in. The gambling world is no place for you, *Sonrisa*, especially when someone you know is in debt. Whenever Whitehorse gambles, there is always trouble."

"That sounds like the reputation of someone else I know," Paige said, crossing her arms and looking around the room.

"I do not run up debt, especially not in a place like this," Miguel said. "You do not want to owe anyone here anything, not money and not favors."

"What makes you think Whitehorse is in debt?"

"He is always in debt," Miguel answered. "He has been gambling all the years I have known him. He tries to quit, but he always goes back. Usually he is trying to win in order to pay his debts off, but this time I think he got in too deep."

"You still didn't tell me who Hector is."

"Hector is his bookie. Whitehorse places his bets through him. But Hector also loans him money to play, which keeps him coming back to the casino. And he expects a lot more back than he loans him, so his debt is never paid off."

"You mean interest," Paige said.

"It is called *vig* in this world," Miguel pointed out. "And it is nothing you want to get involved with."

"And the thugs?"

"They do Hector's dirty work for him."

"Really? Like in the old gangster movies? Like in *Goodfellas*? Like…" Paige's voice trailed off as another cocktail waitress walked by. A good stiff drink was starting to sound good.

"Rosa," Miguel called out, causing the server to turn back.

"I thought you never come here," Paige said. Miguel ignored her.

"Well, if it isn't Miguel himself," the server said, her voice a little too sweet for Paige's taste. "Long time, no see. Did you miss me?"

"Of course, Rosa," Miguel said, flirting back for a moment before becoming serious. "But I am looking for Whitehorse."

"I haven't seen him, not since last night." The waitress was clearly disappointed that Miguel wasn't looking for her. She gave Paige an inquisitive look, but said nothing.

"He was here last night?" Miguel and Paige spoke at the same time.

"Yes, but not for long. He hightailed it out the side door when Hector came around. Did you try down by the trading post?"

"By the..." Miguel looked confused. "By what trading post?"

The server returned Miguel's look, equally confused. "You know, the trading post down by his place, where he sells that jewelry. Beautiful designs. Tiny place, but it's been a popular tourist stop since they opened it a few months ago."

"They?" Again Miguel and Paige spoke at the same time.

"Well, supposedly just Whitehorse," Rosa said. "But everyone knows Hector is behind it. Whitehorse would never have the money to finance a trading post. He spends every dollar he can get his hands on right here in this casino."

"Where is this place?" Paige asked.

"A few miles down the access road to the west," Rosa said, talking directly to Miguel in an obvious move to ignore Paige. "You'll have trouble finding it in the dark. Even in the daylight it looks plain. But you can watch for a light in Whitehorse's trailer, which will be set back on a driveway behind the trading post. If he's there, the light might be on."

"Thanks, Rosa." Miguel reached in his pocket and pulled out a twenty dollar bill, dropping it on Rosa's tray.

"Yeah, thanks for helping *us*, Rosa." Paige barely disguised her sarcasm.

Grabbing Paige's arm again, this time more gently, Miguel pulled her toward the casino's exit.

"You two do not have to fight over me, you know." As usual, Paige could hear the smile in Miguel's voice without even looking.

"Don't even start. Besides, you don't have time for either of us right now." Paige broke free of Miguel's grip for the second time that night and pushed through the door on her own, Miguel trailing behind. "We need to find Whitehorse's place and this trading post. I think the whole situation is starting to look clearer."

CHAPTER TWENTY-FIVE

The door to Room 14 creaked as Paige opened it. Two long hours searching along the frontage roads of Interstate 40 had been in vain. The few roadside stands she and Miguel had seen were boarded up and dark and none matched the description Rosa had given them. Finally, low on gas and worried about pushing too far into the night, Miguel had suggested they turn back to Gallup and begin the search again in the morning when it would be light and easier to see. Reluctantly, Paige agreed.

The Tierra Inn was nothing exciting, but it wasn't horrible, either. Set off to the south of the interstate, the rumbling of eighteen-wheelers promised to be a continuous soundtrack during the night. But the rooms were clean, even quaint, with old Route 66 posters on the walls and ceramic mugs by the coffeemaker, rather than standard Styrofoam motel cups. Even more to Paige's relief, two rooms were available, though Miguel had suggested they share a room to save expenses. Paige had been on the brink of lecturing him when a quick look at his face made it clear he was teasing. "Worth a try," he had murmured on their way out of the office.

Paige set her overnight bag on a carved wooden chair and opened it, pulling out the clothes and toothbrush she'd grabbed before leaving Agua Encantada. She paused to think. Had it only been that morning that she'd gone to Tres Palomas to hear Abuela at the church, then to the Coyote Cantina, then to the spa, then up to Gallup and the casino, then all along the interstate, searching for a trading post and now to the Tierra Inn? It seemed unbelievable she'd done all this in one day.

Changing into pajamas, she tried once more to reach Jake. Again she only got voice mail. There were no new messages since the last one she'd left. *Doesn't he even care enough to check his phone?*

She went to answer a knock on the door. "Paige?" When she opened the door, Miguel began to chastise her. "Do not open this door without making sure you know who it is first," Miguel said, one hand behind his back, the other holding out a mug that matched one of the two in her room.

"I knew it was you. I recognized your voice," she said, though she knew he was right; she should have been more careful.

Miguel's eyes traveled down to take in the bright yellow and white flannel print.

"Don't say a word," Paige warned, watching him fight back half a dozen smart aleck remarks. "I love my rubber ducky pajamas. And is that…?" She took the mug, passed it under her nose and smiled. "Hot chocolate? How did you manage that? I only have coffee in this room."

"I have my ways."

"Meaning you sweet-talked the young girl at the inn's front counter into giving it to you."

"Something like that." Miguel grinned. "Are you going to ask me in or am I going back to my room?" As added incentive, he pulled a bag out from behind his back.

"Food?" Paige's eyes lit up. The day's events had been so intense, she'd forgotten they hadn't eaten.

"Burritos," Miguel confirmed. "Nothing fancy, just what I grabbed at a café half a mile down the road."

"Chips?" Paige asked, as if his answer was the password to stepping inside. She almost felt guilty for letting him stand on the front step this long, holding a hot chocolate in one hand and a dinner offering in the other. With only granola bars in her bag, she wasn't about to pass up the meal.

"And salsa," Miguel said, watching Paige wince. "Mild salsa," he added.

Paige stood back to let him in, taking both the mug of hot chocolate and bag of burritos at the same time. Miguel closed the door and sat at a small table in the corner of the room. Paige placed the bag on the table, pulled out the burritos, chips and salsa and sat down across from him.

"So the trading post – that we can't find – sells jewelry, according to your pal Rosa," Paige said. "I'm guessing that's where Sylvia got her pin, the one with the three silver doves. But I don't understand how Whitehorse got Ana's designs." She dipped a chip tentatively into the salsa and tested it out. "Unless he's been stealing them. Which is a disappointing theory, since I sort of like the old character."

"He hasn't been…."

"Then again, maybe he got desperate," Paige continued, talking over Miguel to keep her momentum going. "You said he has a gambling problem. People with gambling problems do things they might not do otherwise." She wrapped her hands around the burrito and paused, as if she might find the answer by contemplating the generously stuffed tortilla. Shrugging her shoulders, she gave in and took a bite.

"He hasn't been stealing them," Miguel said.

"Miguel, don't be too upset. Sometimes people resort to desperate measures when they're in trouble. It sounds like that's what happened to Whitehorse."

"Yes and no," Miguel said, pushing his food aside. "Yes, he got into trouble. But, no, he hasn't…."

"Actually, that makes sense, then." Paige stood up and paced, stabbing a chip in the air like a teacher pointing at a blackboard. She stopped and turned to Miguel, eyes wide. "That must be who broke into the spa that night last week."

"What are you talking about?" Miguel said, frowning as Paige sat back down.

"You wondered how I knew about breaking into the back of the spa? The first night I was at Agua Encantada, I'm sure I saw a figure lurking around the spa building. And I heard someone inside, too."

"Paige…did you tell anyone?"

"I told Ana, but she said nothing inside the spa had been disturbed," Paige said. "Of course, the wind was fierce that night, which could have caused the moving shadows and the sounds. And a window had come unlatched behind the building."

"Which you just happened to know because you climbed the fence?"

"Uh, yeah," Paige admitted.

"Do you find trouble everywhere you travel?"

"You could say that." Paige dipped another chip in salsa, this time with more confidence. "But what were you trying to tell me a minute ago?"

Miguel stalled, and Paige wondered what was so hard for him to spit out.

"Whitehorse wasn't stealing the jewelry," Miguel said, finally. "He got it from me."

"*You* were stealing it? Your own sister's jewelry?" Paige practically choked on the bite of burrito she'd just taken.

"No, of course I wasn't stealing it!" Miguel said. "Do you really think I would do that?"

Paige looked at him, expressionless. "Miguel, I met you a little over a week ago. I can't be sure what you might or might not do. But you just told me Whitehorse got the jewelry from you, so what am I supposed to think?"

"I thought I was helping sell it," Miguel said. "Whitehorse said he knew some wealthy customers in Santa Fe who wanted the jewelry and were willing to pay more than Ana usually asked for it. So I gave him some pieces to show them. I wanted to surprise her with a great sale. He was supposed to bring me the money the next day."

"But he didn't, did he?" Paige said. "And that's why there was all that tension between you two in the Coyote that day I met Whitehorse. And on the llama trek, too. So…you're the one who broke into the spa that night? To get the jewelry?"

"Yes and no." This time Miguel got up to pace. "I did go into the spa that night, which was stupid of me. I was going to take a few more pieces, thinking Whitehorse might give me the money for all of it. But when I got inside I changed my mind. I did not take anything. I left everything exactly as I found it."

"That's why Ana said nothing was disturbed during the break-in," Paige said.

"Paige, it was not a 'break-in,' you know," Miguel pointed out. "Stop calling it that. I do have keys to all the buildings on the property."

"So when did you give him the first set of jewelry you mentioned."

"A few weeks ago. Why?"

"Because I think I know what Whitehorse is doing. He's having your sister's jewelry duplicated, to sell at his trading post. A few weeks wouldn't be enough time for him to have reproductions made." Paige sipped her hot chocolate and thought it through. "Sylvia only paid eighteen dollars for her pin, which was a copy of one of Ana's designs that sells for seventy, eighty dollars, right?"

"That sounds right," Miguel said. "Whitehorse is supposed to be paying me close to six hundred dollars for the eight designs I gave him."

"He's probably getting them manufactured overseas, then, cheap labor," Paige said. "That takes time. Months, at least. So he must have gotten them from someone else. Who else has access to Ana's jewelry?"

"Lots of people. Agua Encantada is not exactly a high security area. And her jewelry is in the gift shop and Luz's store."

"And some under the counter at the spa," Paige added. "She checked her back stock when I asked her if anything was missing."

"Yes. So anyone could have taken it," Miguel said, stuffing the remnants of their dinner into the bag it came in. "But I know Marisol would not do that, or Luz. No one else works in the lobby or office, and the display case is locked when they are away."

"What about the massage therapist? She told me she works in Luz's shop in the mornings."

"Lena? Maybe," Miguel answered. "I do not know much about her. She only came to Tres Palomas a few months ago."

"And she only works a couple hours each morning?" Paige asked. "Aside from now and then in the spa?"

"Yes, only long enough for Luz to serve breakfast to the resort guests." Miguel frowned, realizing what Paige was already thinking.

"I think we have Whitehorse's other jewelry source," Paige said. She finished her hot chocolate, stood up, held out the mug to Miguel and yawned. It felt like she'd packed three days into one.

"I can take a hint," Miguel said, moving to the door. "Besides, all those ducks are making me a little crazy. I will see you in the morning, early, so we can find the trading post before it opens."

Paige closed and locked the door. She laughed when she heard Miguel quack softly as he walked away. Turning off the lights, she slipped into bed, but a thought nagged at her. Someone was going through a lot of hassle just to supply a trading post with knock-offs of Ana's jewelry designs. There had to be more to the story. As Paige drifted off to sleep, she had a feeling the next day would hold some answers.

CHAPTER TWENTY-SIX

The morning air was still crisp when Miguel knocked on Paige's door the next day. When she didn't answer, he knocked again, a little harder this time. Still no answer. Just as he started to worry, he heard her voice calling him from a distance. Turning, he watched her half-jogging, half-limping toward him from across the parking lot.

"You run?" Miguel asked, his expression a cross between curious and amused.

"Not really," Paige managed, gulping for air as she approached. "In fact, not at all," she admitted as she bent down and placed both hands on her knees.

Miguel crossed his arms and laughed as he waited for her to catch her breath.

"How far do you think you ran?"

"Maybe a quarter of a mile." Paige huffed and puffed.

"Each way?" Miguel pushed on, delighted. He knew her answer.

"No, I'd say that was round trip. And…maybe not that far."

"I am not sure I would call that running," Miguel said. "At least I would not suggest you sign up for any marathons in the near future."

"I woke up early." Paige straightened and stretched one arm over her head, then the other. "I figured it would help me think." She placed her hands on her waist and twisted from side to side, her voice becoming louder and softer as she switched directions.

"Well, did it?"

"Actually, yes," Paige said, sounding surprised herself. "I kept thinking last night that we were missing something and now I'm sure of it. I'll get changed and tell you on the way to Whitehorse's trading post."

"But you're already dressed."

"This is what I wore yesterday. I brought a change of clothes. Meet me at your truck. And let's find some food on our way."

"Food?" Miguel called after her. "You are hungry after that burrito last night?"

"I worked up an appetite running," Paige said as she disappeared into her room.

Thirty minutes later, the two sat across from each other, picking at overcooked scrambled eggs and burnt toast.

"This isn't the New Mexico food I've grown to love during this trip, that's for sure," Paige said. "I wouldn't mind a plate of Luz's *huevos rancheros* about now." She speared a dried out orange slice from the side of the plate and then put it down. "What happened to that burrito place from last night?"

"Not open for breakfast. You wanted food? Truck stop is what you got."

"Fine," Paige said, setting her fork down. "I'm not hungry anyway. Finish your so-called omelet and let's get out of here. I want to find that trading post, see if Abuela's there and then get back to Tres Palomas."

"What was it you were thinking about earlier, while you were running?"

"Just something that was bothering me last night after we talked. You think this is about Whitehorse copying Ana's jewelry and selling the copies as authentic, right?"

"It is not a bad theory, Paige," Miguel said, finishing his omelet and pushing the plate away. "A lot of money is made by passing fake Native American artwork off as authentic."

"No question about that," Paige agreed. "I did some research after Sylvia showed up wearing the pin with Ana's three silver doves design. The annual dollar revenue from sales of Native American art is estimated to be close to a billion dollars. That includes fakes, which are illegal. The Indian Arts and Crafts Act of 1990 established that. It's a truth-in-advertising law."

"Ana is talented and deserves the income for her work, as well as recognition," Miguel said.

"Of course she does," Paige said. "It must hurt to know your own sister is being exploited."

Miguel sighed. "I was an idiot to trust Whitehorse with those pieces. He was never planning to sell them to wealthy customers in Santa Fe."

"Don't be so hard on yourself, Miguel," Paige said. She reached across the table to touch his hand, then hesitated and pulled back. "You were trying to help Ana. That's nothing to be ashamed of."

"I just find it hard to believe Whitehorse used me like that," Miguel continued. "I have known him since I was a child."

"Maybe he didn't do it on purpose," Paige said, leaning back against the ragged vinyl of the booth.

"How do you accidentally take someone's artwork and have it show up mass-produced?" Miguel leaned forward. "He came to *me* with the suggestion that he could help Ana by getting more for her jewelry than she was getting at the resort or at Luz's shop."

"Maybe his gambling problem has gotten worse. Maybe he's being threatened. He was desperate for money to pay off a debt."

"With eight pieces of jewelry?"

"Mass-produced, that could turn into a lot more. Think about the billion dollars of yearly sales," Paige continued. "There's plenty of motivation there, especially if you have debts hanging over your head. And you said he tried to get more samples from you. Plus, it's possible Lena supplied him with more. I wonder if the store's books balance, or if any inventory is missing."

"Marisol does the books for both the resort and the store," Miguel said, pulling money out of his wallet and leaving it on the table to pay the bill. "I'll call her. My cell phone is in the truck. I want to see how Ana is doing, anyway."

"I'll leave a tip and meet you outside." Paige added to what Miguel had left on the table and dug her own cell phone out of her pocket. Not for the first time that morning, she tried Jake's number, to no avail. *Why am I even bothering at this point? Surely he would have returned my calls by now?*

Paige crossed the truck stop parking lot and found Miguel pacing next to his truck. One glance at him told her something was wrong.

"What is it? Is Ana OK?"

"Ana is fine, better after resting yesterday and getting some sleep. Luz had the doctor come out to the resort to check on her. She wasn't hurt physically, just scared."

"That's a relief," Paige said.

"I also asked about the books for the store," Miguel added. "Marisol said everything has always balanced. Whatever jewelry left the store was purchased and paid for." Although what Miguel said sounded like good news, he still looked troubled.

"What else, Miguel," Paige said. "I can tell that's not all."

"The police came out to question Ana and to write a report. They searched the spa building, with Ana's help, so she could identify anything missing. All her jewelry is gone."

"What?" Paige leaned back against the truck. "What about her sketchpad with all her designs?"

"Also gone."

"So this *is* about her jewelry," Paige said. "Then let's get going. We need to find Whitehorse's trading post. Hurry."

Paige opened the passenger door and jumped into the truck. Miguel was right behind her, slamming his door and turning over the ignition at the same time. As the engine fired up, Miguel adjusted the rear view mirror and glanced sideways at Paige.

"Oh, I almost forgot. Marisol said that boyfriend of yours called last night."

"What? Jake called the resort?" Paige said. A queasy feeling began to build in her stomach. "What did she say?"

"She said you'd gone out of town...."

"*And?*"

"That you were with me..."

"*AND?*"

"Not to worry, that we'd be back the next day."

Paige sighed, slumping down and letting her head rest against the truck's seat back. No matter how Jake might have interpreted the conversation with Marisol, it all boiled down to the same conclusion. And it wasn't good.

CHAPTER TWENTY-SEVEN

Paige looked out the windshield of Miguel's truck as he pulled up in front of the unimpressive structure. A sign said "Tierra Trading Post," but nothing resembled the booming jewelry enterprise they'd expected.

Miguel turned off the engine and exchanged glances with Paige.

"Maybe this isn't it," Paige said. "This place would barely hold those eight pieces of jewelry you gave Whitehorse, much less anything else."

"No, this is it," Miguel said. He pointed down the driveway. "You see the truck sticking out behind that trailer? That's Whitehorse's truck."

Miguel backed his truck out of the trading post's parking lot – an area barely large enough to hold four or five cars – and pulled around to the driveway, following it until he reached the trailer. Paige waited in the car as he got out and knocked on the trailer door.

"Whitehorse!" He waited a few seconds before knocking and shouting out again. "It's Miguel, open up!" When he twisted the doorknob, he found it locked.

Paige watched as Miguel walked around the trailer, trying to look in windows. He looked back and shook his head. Circling the trailer once more, he looked under several large rocks, using caution in case anything unwelcome slithered out. Finally he kicked an old gas can aside that rested under one corner of the trailer, lifting up a key, which he flashed in Paige's direction with a triumphant wave. Paige jumped out of the truck and met him at the trailer's door.

"Whitehorse? Abuela?" she yelled, pounding on the door while Miguel inserted the key in the lock. "Hurry up, Miguel," she added. She tried to step in when the door cracked open, but Miguel pulled her back.

"After me," he said. "We don't know who is in here." He stepped inside, Paige only inches behind.

The trailer's interior was dim. Paige pulled open a curtain, coughing as dust flew out from the fabric.

"No one is here," Miguel said, emerging from the only room besides the main area. "There is a mattress and a couple of blankets, but that is all."

"He obviously doesn't spend much time here," Paige noted.

"I never even knew he had property out here," Miguel said. "He spends most of his time in Tres Palomas."

"This must be his crash pad. A place to stay when he comes up here to gamble," Paige suggested.

"We all figured he stayed at the casino. They have rooms in the back for regulars and people passing through town."

Paige walked by Miguel and into the back room, reappearing with an old shawl in one hand. "This is Abuela's, Miguel. I recognize it from last week. She was wearing it during her storytelling session."

"That means she is here," Miguel said.

"Or has been here," Paige added. She moved to each of two other windows, turning her head away to avoid dust as she peered outside. "Nothing...except, you said that's Whitehorse's truck?"

"Yeah, stupid piece of...."

"Then where is Whitehorse?" Paige said. She looked out the window again. "Miguel, look way back there. Is that storage unit on this property?"

Miguel moved to the window, following Paige's gaze. "It might be. Depends on how far back his property goes."

Paige bolted across the trailer. "I'm going to check it out."

"Not alone," Miguel said, following her out the door.

Paige ignored him, already sprinting ahead. Miguel started up the truck and caught up to her, insisting she get in.

"That storage unit is at least one hundred yards down," he shouted. "You ever run a ninety-yard touchdown on a field filled with rattlers?"

Paige stopped abruptly and climbed in the truck.

"City people," Miguel huffed, stepping on the gas.

Paige leaned against the dashboard. As soon as Miguel stopped the truck, she opened her door, paused for a quick look at the ground, then jumped out and ran to the tall metal door. She pounded on the door, calling out Whitehorse and Abuela's names. She placed her ear against the metal, turning quickly as Miguel rushed up behind her.

"I hear something inside," she shouted, startled to find Miguel only inches away. "Scuffling. Someone's in there!"

"Move!" Under different circumstances, Miguel's gruff tone would have been considered rude. He cursed as he yanked on a heavy padlock, then grabbed the edge of the metal door and tried to shake it loose from its hinges.

Paige pressed her ear up against the door again, but only heard the sound of warbling metal.

Miguel ran back to his truck, reaching under the driver's seat and pulled out a crow bar. Returning to the door, he worked the thick metal bar inside the padlock and used his weight to try to pry it open. It didn't budge. He cursed again, adjusting the direction of the pressure. Though the padlock held firm, the latch attached to it began to loosen. Encouraged, he worked the pressure again until he was able to slip the crow bar under the latch itself. With a few grunts, he finally broke the latch's hold. Tossing the crowbar to the side, he wedged himself against the door and pushed it open.

"*Abuela!*" Paige shouted, rushing past Miguel. She pulled a cloth down from the old woman's mouth, ungagging her. "Miguel, help untie her and..." Paige paused, mid-statement. "Lena?"

Miguel pulled a knife from his pocket. Quickly he cut the ropes around Abuela's hands and feet, and then turned toward Lena.

"Do not untie her." Abuela's tone was calm, but firm. Paige and Miguel looked at her, confused.

"Why?" Paige asked.

"She is working with Hector."

"Lena, is that true?" Paige asked.

"So what if it is? A girl's gotta make a living."

Paige lost her temper. "What a despicable thing to do to the people of Tres Palomas! They trusted you!" She continued to spew angry words at Lena until Miguel stepped in.

"Paige, stop it!" Miguel shouted as he turned back to the old woman. "You know Hector, Abuela? How could you know him? He never comes to Tres Palomas."

"No, he does not." Abuela looked straight ahead, solemnly.

"We think he works with Whitehorse," Paige said. "Did you meet him some other time when you came here to visit your brother?"

"I have never been here before," Abuela said.

Now even Lena looked at Abuela, confused.

Paige was the one to ask, "Then how do you know him?"

Abuela faced all three of them, then looked straight ahead.

"Because he is my son."

CHAPTER TWENTY-EIGHT

The main room inside Tierra Roja Casino was lighter in the morning, not so saturated with smoke and monetary seduction as it would be later. Still, it seemed darker to Paige as she entered. Events of the last twenty-four hours weighed heavily on her body and mind. Abuela's rescue had been taxing and her unexpected declaration, shocking. Plus, realizing that Lena was part of Hector's team had shaken her. They still needed to find Whitehorse. And Jake had not returned any of her desperate calls.

"Did you get Abuela settled?" Paige asked Miguel as she scanned the room for any sign of Whitehorse.

"She is in the casino restaurant. I bought her coffee, though she will not touch it."

"That's better than leaving her at the trailer or letting her sit in your truck," Paige said.

"Yes," Miguel agreed. "And I did not want her questioned by Gallup law enforcement when they picked up Lena. The tribal police will have enough questions for her when they arrive here."

"How long will that be?"

"Hopefully, not long. But they will not hurry. There is no actual crime here in the casino, from their viewpoint."

"Then we need to find Whitehorse ourselves." Paige started off in one direction, but Miguel caught up and stopped her.

"Stop, Paige. You cannot search this casino alone, or even with me. Not safely, anyway. You have no idea how dangerous Hector is. Even I did not know until today. I knew he was a bookie; that is no secret to anyone. But the jewelry business and using Whitehorse's property, and his connection to Abuela?"

"Which means Hector is Whitehorse's nephew," Paige pointed out.

"Yes," Miguel said. "So, Hector must have a strong hold over Whitehorse for him to be in this deep."

Paige shook her head. "Like I said this morning, I think there's more to this, which is all the more reason we need to find Whitehorse."

"Then wait for official help, Paige," Miguel said. Reaching out, he placed one hand on Paige's shoulder. "The tribal police will be here soon. This is their job. Please, listen to me."

"Yes, Paige, please listen to him. He obviously has your best interests at heart."

Paige spun around in shock. "Jake! What are you doing here?" Her voice cracked from the combination of stress and anxiety. She brushed Miguel's hand off her shoulder.

"I think a better question is what are *you* doing here? Not to mention *YOU!*" Jake glanced briefly at Miguel, and then back at Paige.

Paige stood mute, caught between Jake's unspoken insinuations and the desire to disappear through the floor. Although the casino wasn't crowded, plenty of customers were still around to witness the scene that was undoubtedly about to unfold. In a rare moment of good judgment, she said nothing.

Instead, Miguel spoke. "Who do you think you are, speaking to this woman like that?" He took a step toward Jake. Paige stopped Miguel by reaching for his arm, a gesture that only made Jake's eyes grow wider.

"Jake! Miguel! Stop it!" Paige yelled.

People in the casino who weren't already staring now turned. Jake and Miguel looked at Paige, who stood, eyes covered, one arm pointing toward the casino's front door. Three tribal police officers approached from that direction.

"Which one of you is Miguel?" The man who spoke was heavyset but muscular, with near-black eyes, and a scar above one eyebrow.

"I am," Miguel answered. "I am the one who called you."

"And is this man helping you?" The officer indicated Jake with a quick glance.

"Hardly," Miguel said, folding his arms.

"We called about Whitehorse," Paige said, turning to the officers.

"And you are?" a second officer asked Paige.

"She is a reporter from New York," Miguel said.

"I work for *The Manhattan Post*, but I'm really here on vacation," Paige said quickly.

"Oh, great," the third officer said. "Just what we need: a reporter. On *vacation*. In our casino."

"Stop it, all of you!" Paige lowered her voice slightly as she realized she was scolding the tribal police along with Miguel and Jake. "We drove from Tres Palomas because the town storyteller didn't show up at church yesterday."

"You drove from that little town all the way here because someone missed church?" All three officers snickered.

Paige turned to the officer who'd asked the question. "Abuela is Charlie Whitehorse's sister. We found her at his property, *bound and gagged,* by the way, in case you still find this situation funny."

Miguel stepped in. "We thinking Hector is holding Whitehorse, most likely here in the casino."

At the mention of Hector's name, all three officers grew serious and listened closely as Miguel explained the situation. He started with the jewelry he'd given Whitehorse and continued through to the discovery of Abuela and Lena in the storage unit.

The lead officer sent the two backup officers to check the casino for Whitehorse. He then escorted Paige and Miguel to the restaurant to get more information from Abuela and from them. Paige asked the officer to let Jake come along. He followed behind, now seeming more bewildered than upset. All took seats around Abuela while the officer took notes.

"I do not want to talk about Hector," Abuela said. "I have nothing to say about him. We have not spoken since he was young, a teenager. He was never a good boy. And he did not become a good man."

"But Whitehorse is your brother," the officer said, taking notes.

"Yes," Abuela said, her gnarled hands clasped together. "He is my brother."

"Then he must have known Hector was his nephew," Paige said, ignoring a disapproving look from the officer as she interrupted.

"Yes, he knew," Abuela said. "But I forbade my brother to speak of him. There is only evil in that boy."

Another radio call came in. The officer took the call and moved outside, leaving Paige, Miguel, Abuela and Jake at the table together.

"Thank you," Abuela said to Paige and Miguel, "for finding me."

"We'll find your brother, too," Paige said, hoping she was right as she reassured the old woman.

"It looks like they did," Miguel said, standing up. The two officers supported Whitehorse between them as they crossed the casino floor toward the exit. Paige gasped at the sight of Whitehorse's badly bruised face. His upper lip was split and crusted with dried blood. One officer helped him out the front door, while the other returned to the group.

"He needs medical help," Paige exclaimed, jumping up from the table.

"Already on the way." The officer held up his hand, indicating there was no need for Paige to rush out.

"What about Hector?" Miguel asked. He had moved over to block Abuela's view, worried that Whitehorse's condition would upset her further.

"Gone, unfortunately" the officer said. "And I'm not sure we'll get anything out of Whitehorse. No one around here wants to cross Hector."

Paige thought she heard the officer clear his throat. *Were even the police afraid of Hector?*

"But we might get information out of that girl, Lena," the lead officer said, clipping his radio into his belt as he walked back in. "That was the Gallup police. They picked her up right where you said she'd be, in that storage shed."

"To think that Lena was involved in this all along," Miguel said, shaking his head. "She was so eager to help in Luz's shop when she moved to Tres Palomas, and she seemed like such a nice girl. Luz was glad to be able to serve breakfast to her guests."

"I'm sure she *was* eager," Paige said. "It was the perfect cover for getting her hands on new jewelry designs."

Paige watched as an ambulance pulled up in front. A tribal officer questioned Whitehorse briefly before letting the medics take him to the hospital to be checked out.

"And Whitehorse thought he was working with Hector alone, but she was in on it from the start," Miguel added. "She thought she had an in with Hector, but no one does."

"That's all I need from any of you," the lead officer said, flipping his notepad closed and sliding it into his front pocket. "If you think of anything else, give me a call." He pulled business cards from his other pocket and handed one to Miguel and then Paige. Hesitating for a moment, he shrugged his shoulders and gave one to Jake, as well.

Miguel turned to Abuela after the officer left. "Come on, I will take you home." With Paige and Jake on each side, he helped her from her chair and led her outside to his truck, opening the door. Abuela climbed in without a word.

Paige was silent as Miguel turned around. The three of them stayed quiet for a moment, none of them wanting to be the first to ask the obvious question.

Finally, Paige said, "Any idea how much a taxi back to Tres Palomas would be? You could split the cost." She crossed her arms and looked from one man to the other, the unspoken cost of a four hour taxi ride hovering between them.

"I'll drive you back," both men said. Paige stood back and let them hash it out.

"I brought her here from Tres Palomas. I will take her back."

"Your truck is crowded. My rental car has lots of room."

Paige shot Jake a frown. That was the best he could come up with? That his car had more room?

"It is my responsibility to take her back."

"It's your responsibility to take *Abuela* back, not Paige."

Paige closed her eyes and counted to five, then opened them and shouted.

"Enough! It's no one's responsibility to take me back to Tres Palomas. I will ride with whichever one of you promises not to say a word to me the whole way."

Instantly Paige regretted the words. Miguel had done nothing to deserve them, and she had to admit that Jake hadn't, either. But the day's experiences had drained her bones of every last ounce of patience.

"I'm sorry," she said. "I'm really tired, and I just want this day to be over." She paused. Considering that a quiet ride back with two other people in the cab of a truck wasn't a ticket to tranquility, she turned to Jake. "If you promise to let me ride in peace, I'll go with you. That means no questions, no comments, nothing until we're back at Agua Encantada."

"Fine," Jake said. "I had a room reserved there last night that would have been much more comfortable than the ratty hole I slept in behind the casino. I'd much prefer that one tonight. Let's go."

"You had a room at Agua Encantada last night?"

"Yes," Jake said. "Until I called for directions from the Albuquerque airport and found out from the office that the two of you were here."

Too exhausted to ask more questions, Paige moved her overnight bag to Jake's rental car, climbed in and buckled her seatbelt. Miguel pulled out onto the highway and headed for the eastbound Interstate 40 onramp. As Jake followed the truck, Paige took headphones out of her bag, plugged them into her cell phone's music stash, put them on and stared out her window until the movement of the car lulled her to sleep.

CHAPTER TWENTY-NINE

The dull tap of Paige's head against the passenger window roused her from sleep. She blinked her eyes, lifted her head and looked out the windshield. A roadway sign noted Albuquerque one hundred miles ahead, so she hadn't slept long. She glanced to her left at Jake, but he was focused on driving and hadn't noticed she was awake. She considered saying something to break the earlier tension, but held her tongue, unsure of what would come out of her mouth. Instead, she turned away and looked back out the window.

Alert now, Paige ran images of the interior of Whitehorse's storage shed through her mind, trying to remember the details. Though small, there had been plenty of empty space. Whatever jewelry enterprise Whitehorse and Hector had going on wasn't filling up even half the shed, in spite of the stacked boxes across the back of the space. The worktable was large. Paige estimated it to be at least eight feet by twelve, allowing plenty of room for sorting and packaging the fake jewelry. There had been a couple of stools alongside the table and the cot that Abuela was sitting on, but otherwise no furniture. With only one light hanging above the table and no windows, the only other light had come from the open front door. There were no other doors. Or were there...?

Paige shot an arm out toward Jake, touching his shoulder.

"Jake, we have to go back." She shifted in her seat to face him, looking over her left shoulder, as if the storage shed was right behind them.

"Please tell me you're kidding," Jake said, keeping his eyes on the road ahead.

"Of course I'm not kidding. There's something we're missing."

"We?" Jake's tone was half irritated and half amused.

"Fine," Paige said, rephrasing her words. "There's something *I'm* missing. And the Gallup police, too." She pointed toward an approaching exit. "There, pull off at that exit up ahead and go back. How long was I asleep? How far are we from Gallup?"

"I'd say you were asleep half an hour," Jake said. "We're probably more than thirty miles from Gallup already."

"I don't care," Paige insisted. "I need to get back to that storage unit."

"On your own? I don't think so, Paige." Jake's voice was firm. "You've managed to get in with gamblers and jewelry smugglers and who knows what else on this trip. You've already found the storyteller you were looking for, so you know she's safe. How about just leaving it alone now?"

"Take the exit." Paige pointed again, ignoring everything Jake had just said. She waved her arm at the off-ramp, fighting the urge to grab the wheel herself.

Jake sighed. "This is against my better judgment. I want that on the record." He signaled and exited the interstate.

"Fine, duly noted" Paige said as the car slowed down and came to a stop. "Now turn left and get back on, going west. We can be back at Whitehorse's place in twenty minutes."

"Thirty minutes," Jake corrected.

"The speed limit here is eighty," Paige said.

"Seventy-five," Jake said, correcting her again.

"Close enough." Paige tapped her fingers on the dashboard.

It took just under thirty minutes to arrive in Gallup and another ten to find Whitehorse's property. Jake pulled the rental car up beside the trailer. Paige jumped out and knocked on the door, expecting the home to be empty. The muffled "come in" surprised her

"Why aren't you at the hospital?" Paige looked at Whitehorse, shocked to see him on his mattress, a bag of ice against his bruised face.

"No broken bones, no insurance," he muttered. "They patched me up and sent me home. I just got back here a few minutes ago." He winced, moving the bag of ice to a different spot on his face.

"Did you talk to the police?" Paige said. "What did they say?"

"Stay away from the casino and get a good lawyer."

"Keep the ice on," Paige said. "I just want permission to go back inside the storage shed."

"Go ahead. Nothing in there but a bunch of jewelry. Hector put the shed up and he handled the business. That was a mistake. I never should have let Hector use this property, but...." Again he winced.

"Don't try to talk anymore," Paige insisted. "I'll check in on you before we leave."

"Miguel's here?"

"No, Jake. Miguel took your sister home."

"Who's Jake?

"I'll explain later. Just rest."

Paige ran back to the car, finding Jake standing outside, leaning against the driver's side. She motioned to him to get in as she opened the passenger door.

"We could walk," he said. "It's not far."

"Rattlesnakes," Paige said, climbing into the vehicle.

"Rattlesnakes?" Jake asked, getting in and starting up the engine.

"You don't have them in Jackson Hole?"

"Altitude is too high. Wyoming has rattlers, but at lower elevations."

Jake pulled the car up in front of the storage unit, barely rolling to a stop before Paige jumped out. The police had tied the metal door closed with rope, presumably when they picked up Lena. But the latch that Miguel had pried open that morning still hung loose, one strand of rope looped through a hole in the metal. Paige tugged on the rope, attempting to untie it, but the knot held firm.

"Do you have that pocket knife of yours..." Paige shouted the question to Jake without turning to see that he'd walked up behind her. She looked over her shoulder and lowered her voice. "...with you?" With this unexpected closeness, his face so near, she could feel her anger crumbling.

Jake thrust his hand in his pocket, pulling out a penknife. "I'm not sure this is a good idea, Paige. If the police tied this shut, it should probably stay that way."

"Do you see a police sign anywhere? Whitehorse said we could check out the storage unit and this is his property. Seems to me we aren't breaking any laws." She took the knife from Jake and pried it open, working swiftly to slice through the rope. As the door fell open, she handed the knife back to Jake. Stepping inside, she headed straight for a closet door in a far corner and tried to open it. *Locked. Of course.*

Jake followed Paige into the shed, looked at the stacks of boxes and then turned his attention to the worktable. "What is all this?"

Paige moved to the table, picked up a clipboard, looked it over and set it back down. "Look." She held up a large plastic bag and dumped the contents out. Dozens of silver pins spread across the table, each one wrapped individually in more clear plastic.

"I don't understand." Jake said. "These can't be that valuable."

"That's not exactly true," Paige said. "The Native American jewelry trade is bigger than you'd think. It's a billion dollar business."

"OK, so you're saying a lot of money is tied up in here. But all this for that little shack of a trading post in front?" Jake pointed at the stacks of boxes. "That's a lot of inventory."

Paige shook her head and pointed to the clipboard. "It's not all for here. They've been shipping it out to trading posts all over the state. And look at the boxes." Paige pulled an empty carton from under the table. "This jewelry is being manufactured overseas, but is being passed off as authentic."

"So you think this is tied to the artist at Agua Encantada?"

"I know it is," Paige said, holding up one of the pieces. "Look at this design with three doves. It's Ana's. This is the pin that Sylvia was wearing, the woman from the tour group I told you about. She said she purchased it somewhere on I-40. And her receipt says 'Gallup.' I'm sure she bought it here. I'd bet every one of those boxes has Ana's designs, all being sold as handmade Native American art, but all fakes."

"OK, I get it, Paige," Jake said, running his hand through his hair. "But let the police take it from here. You always get attached to local people on your trips and end up getting in over your head. Now you're in the middle of some sort of dangerous family feud. And you're mixed up in illegal imported goods, which are somehow tied to Whitehorse's bookie and the casino here, which is a bad sign to begin with. You saw what these people did to Whitehorse. It's time to walk away. I don't think you understand the mess you've gotten into this time."

Paige placed both hands on the table and leaned forward. "No, Jake. *You* don't understand. These are good people and I'm *not* walking away. Besides, this isn't why I made you turn back."

"I was afraid of that."

"There's still something else going on here."

"Another thing I was afraid of."

Paige ducked below the table, searching the lower surface with her hands.

"What are you looking for?"

"A key to that door in the corner. I think the shipping supplies are kept in there." Paige stood up, put her hands on her hips and looked around. "It has to be here somewhere." She ran her hands under both stools, moving on to inspect the cot. Not finding anything, she began circling the room, inspecting the walls.

"Who handled the shipping?" Jake followed Paige as she searched the walls. "That Hector guy? Or someone who works for him, maybe the same person who beat up Whitehorse?"

"Maybe," Paige said. "But why didn't he just have Lena do the shipping, too? Though I guess that wouldn't make sense. She was in Tres Palomas. In fact, I don't even understand why she was here at all. Obviously she was the connection for getting Ana's designs to Hector. Why wouldn't she just stay there to pass on new ones?"

"Whitehorse could be confused, Paige," Jake pointed out. "He took a bad beating. Or he could be lying."

"Why would he lie?" Paige moved on to a pile of boxes, checking the floor around them and feeling the cracks between each stacked box. She finished one row and moved on to the next. "I don't think Whitehorse had any idea what he was getting into this time. Plus, Hector obviously was using his relationship as added leverage somehow."

Paige moved to the next stack of boxes. "He believed giving Hector the jewelry was going to get him out of trouble. He gave him the designs and the use of his property. Hector promised him that would clear his debt. I don't think he would have gotten into it, otherwise...." She stopped speaking abruptly, occupied with maneuvering one box off of the one below it. As Jake moved around beside her, she slid her fingers under the edge of the upper box, pulling out a metal key that had been wedged between the cardboard layers.

"This is it," she said, holding the key up briefly before heading across to the door. She inserted the key and attempted to twist it in the lock, but it didn't budge. She pulled the key out and tried again, with no luck.

"That's odd," she said, staring at the key as if doing so would make it work. "Why would this key be here if not to open that closet? The only other door here is in front, which is locked with a padlock. It uses a different sort of key."

"Maybe it's a spare key to Whitehorse's trailer?"

"I don't think so," Paige said. She swiveled on her heel and walked to the storage unit's exit with Jake following.

"Now what, Paige? Just leave the key. It doesn't fit the closet lock. Let me take you back to Tres Palomas now."

"Not yet." Paige climbed into the car. "I want to ask Whitehorse about the key. He might recognize it, even if it isn't his. Hurry." Jake sighed as he climbed into the driver's seat and started the car. In minutes they were back at the trailer.

Paige tapped on the trailer door before letting herself in. She found Whitehorse exactly where she'd left him, his half-thawed ice pack now pressed over his forehead and eyes.

"Do you have any more ice, Whitehorse?" Paige said.

"In the freezer…"

Paige gently peeled the ice pack from Whitehorse's forehead, drained the water in his sink and filled it with ice from the battered metal trays in the freezer.

"There you go," she said as she handed him the new pack.

"Thank you kindly."

"Can I ask you about something?"

"Yes, ma'am." Whitehorse sighed as he pressed the freshened pack against his jaw.

"Take a look at this key. Do you recognize it?"

He frowned and shook his head, wincing at the movement.

"I thought it would open the closet in the back corner of the storage unit," Paige said, "but the key just stuck in the lock. The doorknob wouldn't turn."

Whitehorse looked at the key again. "Did you try the outside door?"

"The front door?" Paige asked. "There's a padlock on that. It takes a smaller key."

"No, I mean in the back." Whitehorse shifted his position, wincing again. "There's a door at the back of the storage unit."

Paige looked out the trailer's window at the storage unit. She paused, looked at the key, and then back up.

"Thank you, Whitehorse. I hope you feel better soon and that this mess gets cleared up."

Paige returned to the car and directed Jake back down the driveway. Knowing better than to argue with her, he parked behind the storage unit.

"There," Paige said. Once out of the car, she had the key in the lock in seconds. As Jake caught up with her, she pulled the door open and stopped.

"There's nothing in here but a rake and a few other garden tools," Jake said.

"That doesn't make sense. Why hide the key, then?" Paige stepped inside the shallow area. "Unless...." She placed her hands on the back wall.

"Unless what?"

"Unless it's not just tool storage," she said. "That back closet extended out how far inside? About eight feet, I think. And this is only three feet deep or so." Pushing against the wall, she could feel it move. "Jake, this is a false back! I'm sure of it."

Jake stepped forward and reached along one side, stopping part way down and pulling his knife out again. Slipping it inside, he applied pressure until a large panel fell forward, revealing an extended area of several feet. Shelves lined each side, boxes on some and metal bins on others.

"There's no light," Paige said, feeling along the walls. "And there's no door on the back, but we saw one from the inside."

"Which means...." Jake began.

"Which means there's a false wall on each side. What does that tell you, Jake?"

Jake cleared his throat. "It tells me we shouldn't be in here."

Paige pulled her cell phone out of her pocket and, using it as a flashlight, scanned the shelves.

"Jake, look at the names on these bins – Deming, Santa Teresa. They match the packing list destinations on that clipboard inside."

"Deming? Santa Teresa?" Jake repeated. "I thought the shipments were going to trading posts along the interstate."

"They are," Paige said. "But some are going south, too. Why does that matter?"

"Because those are..." Jake's voice grew muffled as he reached up to the top shelves, his height an advantage. "Those are border routes," he said, grabbing the cell phone from her and using the light to inspect the contents of a metal bin.

As Jake turned back to face her, Paige gasped. The plastic bag of powder he held needed no explanation, but he gave one, anyway.

"And this, Paige, is not jewelry."

CHAPTER THIRTY

The heavy-set man in his mid-forties who stood behind the front desk of the Gallup Police Department looked up from a file when Paige and Jake burst through the door.

"What can I do for you folks? I'm Officer Hernandez."

Paige rushed into an explanation: "We found Whitehorse's trailer and the storage unit and discovered Abuela and Lena were tied up, so we helped Abuela then we went to the casino because Abuela told us Hector took Whitehorse, and the tribal police found Whitehorse, all beaten up, but he'll be OK, so we left to take Abuela home to Tres Palomas but I realized I'd missed something at the storage unit so we turned around and came back to Gallup, and we found...."

"Whoa! Slow down and back up a minute," the officer said. "You're the ones who found Lena at Whitehorse's place?"

"No, Miguel and I found her, along with Whitehorse's sister, the storyteller from Tres Palomas. But we missed something in our rush to get to the casino to find Whitehorse...."

The officer turned his attention to Jake, stopping Paige again. "So if you're not Miguel, and you didn't find Lena, who are you?"

"Jake Norris, a…" he paused slightly. "A friend of Paige's from Wyoming."

Paige shot him a frown. *A friend?*

"And who is Miguel?" The officer directed this question to Paige.

"He works at Agua Encantada resort. I'm staying there."

"The term 'staying there' being relative, clearly," Jake added, earning another frown from Paige. *Was she imagining a smile on the officer's face?*

"Do you have Lena here, in custody?" Paige asked. "We didn't free her because Abuela told us she was involved in Hector's illegal scheme, but we called the police before going to the casino."

"Lena is here," Officer Hernandez said, "though not in custody."

"Well, she should be," Paige insisted. "She was helping commit a crime." *What was wrong with this police bureau?*

"How about I let you talk to her?" The officer stepped aside as Lena walked up to replace him. Paige's eyes grew wide. Instead of the woman from the storage shed in rumpled clothing or the prisoner in jailbird garb Paige expected, Lena stood before her in a police officer's uniform.

"Hello, Paige," Lena said. She glanced at Jake, but said nothing. "Why don't you come around to my office?" Following Lena's directions, Paige and Jake entered the administrative area through a side door. A long hallway led to the back of the station. Paige stifled the impulse to smile as they passed a side table with coffee and donuts along the way. Jake nudged her, to keep her from commenting on the stereotypical police snack.

"So, Lena…." Paige said, trying to gather her jumbled thoughts as they settled into a back office.

"It's actually Detective Ramirez, but you're welcome to call me Lena." Lena smiled as she turned to reach into a drawer for a notepad. Paige could see bruises along her cheekbone and neck. An image of Lena, tied up in the storage unit, came back at her.

"Oh!" Paige gasped. "I said some awful things to you this morning!" She turned to Jake, who simply shook his head.

To Paige's relief, the detective laughed. "Yes, I believe you called me a low-life scumbag or something equally vicious. I'd say, on a 1 to 10 scale of things I've been called while undercover, that doesn't even merit a 2. Trust me."

"Paige is ruthless when she's on a quest," Jake quipped. He leaned forward in his chair, resting his elbows on his knees, hands clasped. "A force to be reckoned with." Paige had an urge to touch his tan, muscular forearms.

"I've noticed that." Lena jotted something on the notepad. Paige leaned forward to try to read it, but sat up straight when Lena looked up. "So, Paige and..." She paused, looking over at Jake.

"Jake."

"Jake," Lena noted. "As you now see, I've been working undercover on this case for some time. Paige, you came to Gallup with Miguel to find Abuela, the storyteller, correct?"

Paige nodded, trying to formulate the rest of the story in her head so it would make sense when she explained it.

"And you found her, basically unharmed." Lena continued. "I believe Miguel is taking her back to Tres Palomas as we speak. And I know you found Whitehorse, or the tribal police did, since they called us. Which leads me to ask, why are you still here?"

Paige shifted uncomfortably in her seat.

"You're right, we came down here to find Abuela, but also because someone broke into the spa and tied up Miguel's sister, and he was upset. He thought Whitehorse would know where Abuela was and would know something about the break-in, and I insisted on coming along." Paige paused, ignoring the feeling of Jake's eyes drilling into the side of her face. "But, wait…didn't you…?"

Lena nodded. "Yes, I called to say I was opening for Ana so that Hector's sidekick could get in to take her back stock of jewelry – a necessary move to gain his trust and get inside his warehouse. I was going to stall Ana at Luz's store. Her usual pattern was to stop by each morning to get paid for any pieces that had sold the previous day. But she went to work early and was already inside the spa when he arrived. She shouldn't have been in the middle of it. That was a case of bad timing."

"So you hadn't even been inside the warehouse until yesterday?"

"That's correct," Lena said. "I'd been working from Tres Palomas until then, getting closer to Hector by passing jewelry through Whitehorse."

"But Marisol said the books always balanced," Paige said.

"Yes, they would have," Lena said. "Whitehorse always paid for the pieces, as well as extra money that I kept. Hector told him to do that. It made me an accomplice in their eyes because I was pocketing additional money for myself. I gained credibility."

Paige leaned forward in her chair. "Then you'd only just gotten to the storage unit before we arrived? You hadn't searched the place?"

"I didn't get a chance to. I'd barely been dropped off when Abuela came wandering in and made herself comfortable. I sorted some jewelry on the worktable, hoping she'd leave, but then Whitehorse came in, and Hector, behind him."

"And Hector turned on you," Paige said. "So you weren't able to look around."

"Exactly," Lena said. "Months of preparation can be blown simply when one person gets in the way."

Jake coughed. Paige ignored him.

Lena's expression grew serious. "But why are you asking if I searched the place?"

"Because I did…we did." Paige amended the comment, indicating Jake.

"You went *back there*? To Whitehorse's property?" Now Lena was the one leaning forward. "This isn't your business, Paige. Aren't you supposedly here on vacation? And to write an article on the mineral springs?"

"Both," Paige said, matching Lena's tone. "But I care about Ana's designs getting stolen. The fake jewelry trade is a serious problem."

"That's true," Lena conceded. "But that's an ongoing problem we work with every day. You can leave that to us."

"I was also worried about Abuela," Paige continued, "as well as Miguel driving alone when he was upset. But I went *back there* because I knew we'd missed something, which is what we came here, to report…."

"That's private property," Lena interrupted.

"Whitehorse gave us permission to go in." Paige countered.

"He shouldn't have," Lena said.

"Paige…" Jake said, trying to cut her off.

"Well, he did," Paige continued. "And it's a good thing, since your little jewelry operation is covering up something much bigger."

"You have excellent instincts, Paige," Lena said sternly, cutting Paige off again. "You probably missed your calling. But you don't belong in the middle of this."

"But you're not listening," Paige said, confused. "We came down here to…."

Lena stood up abruptly and forced a smile. "I'm politely asking you to go back to Tres Palomas and leave this alone. In fact, maybe returning to New York would be a good idea." She glanced at Jake, a plea for backup.

"Paige!" Jake shouted this time, finally getting her attention.

"What?" Paige shouted back, her face angry as she turned toward Jake.

"Paige, I'm afraid *we're* the ones not seeing the big picture." Jake looked over at Lena, earning a nod of approval, before turning back to Paige. "This undercover operation you've walked in on? That *we've* now walked in on?"

"Right," Paige said, indicating Lena's uniform. "I think that's obvious."

"Yes, it's obvious," Jake said, "except for one thing. Think about it."

Paige sat back, silent for a moment and then covered her mouth, glancing between Jake and Lena as the realization sunk in. She dropped her hand to her lap and spoke. "This undercover operation was never about jewelry, was it?"

Lena shook her head. "Now will you go back to Tres Palomas?" Lena's voice was firm, but kind.

Paige nodded, shook Lena's hand and left with Jake.

CHAPTER THIRTY-ONE

Four hours after leaving Gallup, Paige and Jake pulled into Agua Encantada, hungry and weary. They were relieved that they hadn't missed dinner, and headed straight into the café, where they sat at a corner table, away from other guests.

Luz brought glasses of ice water, along with a basket of chips. "You two look all tuckered out. What about some Indian tacos on fry bread to boost your energy?"

"Definitely!" Paige said. "You'll love them, Jake. I've loved everything Luz has served since I've been here."

After Luz left them, an awkward silence fell.

Paige watched Jake study the artwork and decorations she had admired when she'd first arrived. *Was that only ten days ago?* It felt like she'd been there a solid month.

"Who's that with Miguel, over there?" Jake's eyes settled on another table, where Miguel and Marisol whispered as she placed a serving of flan in front of him.

"That's Marisol. She works the front desk." Paige dipped a chip into salsa and took a crunchy bite.

"Ah, yes. I've talked to her on the phone. Looks like Miguel's flirting with her."

"He flirts with everyone," Paige laughed.

"With everyone…?"

With those two words, Paige heard the tone of Jake's voice turn from baffled to embarrassed. She said nothing, reaching, instead, for another chip. But she smiled.

Jake sighed. "I've acted like a fool while you've been on this trip, haven't I?"

"A little," Paige admitted. "But I have, too." They paused as Luz placed plates with tacos in front of them, large rounds of fry bread underneath stacks of beans, cheese, tomatoes and lettuce.

Paige pushed the salsa toward Jake. "Add some of this. Luz makes it from scratch every day."

Jake took a small spoonful and dribbled it on one side of his plate.

"Oh, take more. It's delicious," Paige said, raising her voice enough to carry. She glanced over and caught Miguel watching Jake add a heftier amount directly on his meal. Miguel winked at Paige. Marisol rolled her eyes.

As Jake took a generous bite, Paige nudged his water glass closer to his plate. He grabbed it almost immediately, gulping down half the glass at once.

When he came up for air, he said, "I suppose I deserved that."

"I just thought I'd share one of my experiences from my first days here. Can you breathe?" He nodded. "Good. So. What brings you all the way to Tres Palomas, Jake Norris?"

"I wanted to see you," he said, pushing some of the salsa off the taco. "And to talk to you. But not now, later."

Paige's stomach knotted around her first bite of dinner. *Is this a good thing or a bad thing? A good thing, right?*

Following Jake's cue, Paige kept the conversation light, telling him about the resort's special pools, the options to get massages or take mud baths. She told him about the town, about the southwestern cuisine and about Abuela's stories.

Finishing up the meal, they both declined dessert and left the café, stopping at the front desk for the key to a casita Jake had reserved before flying down. Paige glanced at the key to the separate accommodation, both relieved and nervous. Having a "talk" was one thing. *Anticipating* a talk was something else.

At his rental car, Jake retrieved Paige's overnight bag and walked her to her casita.

"How about meeting at 9 o'clock?" *Tonight?* "It's 8 o'clock now. That gives you an hour to regroup. I'll come get you." *Ah, yes, he does mean tonight....*

Paige opened the door to her room and paused to look back at Jake. Just seeing him walk away, she knew in her heart which way she hoped the talk would go. She stepped inside, closed the door and leaned her forehead against it. *Was I too harsh on the phone? Is the long distance thing too much for him?*

The hour passed too slowly and too quickly, as if the clock and her heart were at odds. She showered, dried her hair and changed clothes a half dozen times, finally choosing a favorite, sleeveless cotton dress. The loose, button-down style was casual, yet flirtatious, flattering. And the aqua print complimented the auburn highlights in her hair. Sliding into sandals, she paused and switched to flats, in case they ended up walking around the dusty property. She applied a quick touch of make-up and slipped on Ana's earrings, admiring the dangling motion of three silver doves below each ear. Then she paced.

Even though she was expecting the knock on her door, she jumped when it came at 9 o'clock. Taking a deep breath, she calmed her nerves and opened the door.

Marisol?

Her heart dropped. *He changed his mind. He backed out. Whatever it was he wanted to talk about, he decided against it.*

Marisol smiled. "You'll want to wear a swimsuit under that. At least, I think so."

Flustered, Paige grabbed her swimsuit, changing quickly in the bathroom, grateful she'd chosen a dress that could double as a bathing suit cover-up. Changing six more times to find another outfit would have been more than she could handle. This was as stressful as searching for Abuela.

She returned to Marisol and stepped outside, closing the door behind her.

"You two are making me nervous," Paige whispered as she walked beside Marisol, letting her lead her across the property.

"Don't be," Marisol said. She smiled and touched Paige's elbow, turning her toward the private mineral springs. "Go...you'll know which one."

Why do I feel like I'm on an episode of The Bachelor? Paige thought as she walked up the pathway. *Am I getting a rose or being sent home? Stop being ridiculous! You're a grown woman and this is not a television show!*

As she approached the fences that set the individual mineral pools apart for privacy, she could tell where she was headed, just as Marisol had said. While the other enclosures remained dark, one glowed faintly. She stopped at the edge of the fencing in a futile attempt to calm herself. *I could still turn back...* She knew she had to go forward. She rounded the corner and looked inside.

The sparkling reflections of votive candles danced on the water's surface. How many were there? Fifty? One hundred? Had she ever seen so many candles lit up at once? At one end of the pool, a bottle of champagne sat in a silver ice bucket, two glasses alongside. On one wall, two plush bathrobes hung on wrought iron hooks. The soft breeze blowing across the remote New Mexico landscape was soft background music to the enchanting scene. And, at the far end of the private enclosure, sitting at the edge of the pool, was Jake.

At a loss for words, Paige waited as Jake stood up and walked around the pool, each step bringing him closer, each second causing Paige's breathing to quicken. The candlelight framed his silhouette as he approached. Had Paige not known better, she might have thought it was a vision. This was the stuff of movies, of romance novels: a handsome cowboy, sculpted muscles beneath an open shirt, eyes focused on her, twenty feet away, then ten, then five, then...

Warmth rushed through her as Jake slipped one hand around her waist and placed the other alongside her face, his thumb caressing her cheek softly. His eyes never left hers, even as he moved his hand from her waist to her forehead, where he brushed away a windblown strand of hair. As he cupped both hands around her face, Paige closed her eyes, fighting what felt like vertigo. A voice somewhere in the back of her mind told her to lift her arms toward him, but she found herself unable to move. She could feel his warm hands on her skin, the closeness of his breath on her face. As his thumbs stroked her cheeks, she felt his lips press softly against her forehead, then move down to her eyelid and alongside her face. Paige gasped slightly as his lips brushed past her ear and onto her neck. He whispered her name and traced the outline of her face and neck with his fingers, moving on to the buttons down the front of her dress. One by one, he unbuttoned them, his eyes never wavering from hers as he slipped the dress off her shoulders, letting it fall on the ground.

Jake glanced down and grinned. "Swimsuit, how very wise."

"Marisol warned me," Paige whispered, barely finding her voice. She smiled.

Taking Paige's hand, Jake guided her to the far end of the mineral pool, leading her cautiously around the votive candles. She placed her hands against his chest and followed the contours of his muscles upward, slid his shirt off his shoulders. Trailing her fingertips down along his tight abdominal muscles, she hesitated only a split second before he leaned forward and whispered in her ear.

"Swim trunks..." Jake stepped back and winked at her. "Marisol warned me." Paige covered her face, embarrassed at her own shyness. Jake took off his jeans, dropped them on the lounge chair, and then eased her into the mineral springs, one step at a time.

If not for the brisk, evening breeze, Paige might have fainted from the combination of steaming water and her heightened senses. Instead, she let the cool air on her face soothe her as she sat back against the rock surface that formed the side of the pool, Jake by her side.

"You came all the way to Tres Palomas from Jackson Hole just to surprise me with this tonight?" Paige kept her eyes closed, the back of her neck resting against the edge of the pool. She heard Jake chuckle.

"Actually, I came all the way to surprise you with this *last* night."

"Oh," Paige admitted. "I guess that's right." She cringed a little. *He does have a point there.*

"And then when I called from the Albuquerque airport to get directions here..."

"I'm sorry." Paige stopped him. She didn't even want to think about what must have gone through his mind when Marisol told him she was out of town with Miguel. "I know how that must have looked. But..."

"I know, Paige," Jake said, turning to face her, setting off tiny ripples in the water. "I jumped to conclusions." He leaned forward, placing one arm alongside her shoulder, against the pool's edge, and running the back of his other hand across her cheek.

"Well," Paige admitted. "In retrospect, that was sort of flattering." She smiled. With her head still back, eyes still closed, she didn't need to look at Jake to know he was smiling, too.

"Yes, I suppose it was." Jake laughed lightly. "But that's not the only reason I came down here to see you."

Paige felt the butterflies start up again. She had an urge to freeze time. *Everything is perfect right now. Please don't say anything to break this spell...*

"I came down here to Tres Palomas because I wanted to tell you something," Jake said. "And I wanted to tell you in person. It only felt right." *Here we go. This is where I get sent home without a rose...*

Paige felt him move closer, his chest brushing against hers as he placed tiny kisses on her neck. The soft lapping of the water, the cool evening breeze and the sensation of his lips against her skin were almost too much.

"I've been thinking about you, about us, ever since that phone call last week." Jake paused, the soft kisses stopping. "And I had no right to react the way I did. We've never defined our relationship." *Ah, he said the "r" word...is this a good sign or bad?*

Paige lifted her head and looked at Jake, the candlelight reflecting just enough to pick up the blue in his eyes. She held her breath as he cupped his hands around her face. He spoke with a tone more serious than she'd heard from him the entire time she'd known him.

"Paige MacKenzie," he said, "you are the most stubborn, independent, driven, pig-headed, infuriating woman I've ever known."

"I know," Paige whispered. She tried to look away, but Jake's hands held firm, his eyes locked on hers.

"And I don't want you to change, ever." Jake took a deep breath and continued. "Because I love you, Paige, exactly the way you are."

"You…" Paige whispered, unable to form a sentence. She could feel tears forming.

"Yes, I love you," Jake repeated softly, moving one hand away from her face to tuck a lock of hair back behind her ear.. "That's what I came to Tres Palomas to tell you. I needed to tell you in person. And it doesn't matter how you feel, or where you want this to go, or even if you don't want it to go anywhere, I just wanted you to know…and…Paige…why are you crying?"

Jake's confusion was so endearing, Paige started to laugh on top of the tears, a combination that soon turned into hiccups. *Leave it to a guy to not understand tears of joy.*

"Jake," she said, managing to rein in her emotions. "I'm crying because I feel the same way."

With an expression of mock seriousness, Jake pulled back. "You think I'm stubborn, pig-headed and infuriating?"

"Only occasionally," Paige laughed. "But these tears are because I feel the same, Jake. I never expected you when I came out for that first assignment in Jackson Hole, but there you were, sitting in the Blue Moon Café, crashing into me at the library…"

"Uhm…" Jake interrupted, placing one finger against Paige's lips. "I believe *you* crashed into *me*."

"Whichever." Paige shrugged and smiled. "The point is, I love you, too, Jake. I'm not interested in Miguel or anyone else. I want to see where this goes."

Jake leaned forward and brushed his lips against hers, first gently and then more passionately. He lifted her up and drew her close, wrapping his arms around her. As they pulled away from the kiss, Paige leaned against his chest; her head nestled into a perfect resting place beneath his chin.

Casting a glance at the shimmering votive candlelight that surrounded the pool, she closed her eyes and felt the cool breeze caress her shoulders. She'd hoped to find something special in Tres Palomas, just as she did on each assignment – insight into the area, the people and, in the process, into herself. But, wrapped up in Jake's strong arms, she knew she'd found far more on this trip. She'd found home.

CHAPTER THIRTY-TWO

Luz placed a plate of blue corn pancakes in front of Paige, setting a small pitcher of prickly pear syrup in the middle of the table.

"Paige requested this breakfast," Luz said, placing a matching serving in front of Jake, "so you could taste our blue corn pancakes. I'm sure you have pancakes up there in Wyoming, but not like these."

Jake poured syrup on his plate and took a bite, nodding his approval. "Wonderful, Luz."

"You must also have our scrambled eggs." Marisol set another plate on the table. Jake looked at the serving dish curiously.

"Cheddar cheese, green chiles, tomatoes and cilantro," Miguel explained as he slid into a chair at the table. He poured a glass of orange juice from a tall pitcher and rubbed his hands together eagerly as Luz set a plate of pancakes in front of him. Paige said a silent prayer of thanks that Jake and Miguel had run into each other earlier that morning, while loading Paige's luggage into her rental car. They'd gotten all the apologetic handshakes and back slaps out of the way without her having to be in the middle of it.

"How is Abuela?" Paige asked Marisol, who was now filling coffee mugs from a carafe.

"Getting settled again, according to Padre Juan," Marisol said. "The police took a statement. She refused to press any charges. Whitehorse never meant her any harm, and Hector, well, that's obviously a long story. She won't talk about it and he'll be locked away for years. The police finally caught up with him down by the Mexican border."

"What about Whitehorse?" Paige asked, turning to Miguel. "How heavy handed will the police be with him?"

Miguel took a generous bite of pancakes and waited until his mouth was clear to speak. "I think they will go easy. Hector was blackmailing him with threats to hurt Abuela and using him to provide a cover for his drug smuggling and distributing. Whitehorse did not know about the drugs. Without knowing it, he gave the police a way to solve a bigger problem. By following the jewelry trail, they took apart a drug operation."

"He did take Ana's jewelry, though," Paige pointed out.

"True," Miguel said. "But he intended to pay her for it. And he did not know Hector was going to mass-produce copies at first. Once he realized it, he was in too deep to get out."

"And Ana's designs?" Jake asked, helping himself to a second serving of eggs.

Miguel sighed. "Padre Juan recommended a good lawyer up in Santa Fe. She should be able to get damages. The trading posts selling the jewelry knock-offs were all making money from them, but most have been closed down now because of the drugs. A few were not involved in the drug running. It is too early to tell how that will play out. The police are confiscating any jewelry still in stock."

"But those designs are already out there, without Ana getting credit for them," Luz said as she replaced the empty platter of pancakes in the center of the table with a full one.

"I talked to her this morning," Paige said, smiling. "She's not bothered by the ones people already bought, 'since they will be enjoyed,' she told me." Paige pictured Sylvia's pin. The idea of others enjoying the designs wasn't a bad thought.

"You'll need to hire a new shop person now, Luz," Jake said.

"Yes," Luz admitted. "Padre Juan will announce that on Sunday. It's too bad, though. Lena was great in the store, not to mention popular with guests in the spa. It's a shame she has to go back to her real job."

"Someone has to catch the bad guys, you know," Miguel pointed out. "Though I still find it hard to believe she was working undercover, right here in Tres Palomas and no one suspected." He shook his head.

"What time is your flight?" Marisol asked Paige.

"Not until 4:30 this afternoon," Paige said, "though I should get up to Albuquerque early. I need to leave here by noon."

"We're going to miss you, Paige," Luz said. "This town hasn't been the same since you arrived."

"Funny thing, that tends to happen wherever Paige goes," Jake said. Paige grinned.

"I think Rico will miss you the most," Miguel added. He winked at Paige when Jake's eyebrows lifted.

"You're right," Paige said solemnly. "I'll miss him, too. A lot." She looked at Jake apologetically.

Miguel glanced back and forth between Paige and Jake. "Paige," he whispered, barely loud enough for Jake to hear. "Did you not tell Jake about Rico?"

Paige sighed, playing along. "I couldn't Miguel, I just couldn't."

"Time to come clean, Paige," Miguel said, standing up. "Better go introduce them to each other."

"Whatever you two are up to, I'm not falling for it." Jake pushed his plate away, full from having seconds of everything.

"Come with us," Paige said, looking at Miguel, who shook his head.

"No, you go ahead. I need to run into town for supplies to fix that back window in the spa building."

Paige stood up and picked up her plate without thinking, ready to take it to the kitchen. Marisol stopped her.

"Just leave that," Marisol said. "You feel more like family to us now, but you're still a guest. I'll clean up. Go on out to introduce Jake to Rico."

Reluctantly, Paige left her plate on the table. The staff at Agua Encantada *did* feel like family. She already knew saying goodbye would be hard, not to mention the goodbye she'd need to say to Jake at the airport.

She pushed those thoughts aside and motioned to Jake, who followed her as she led him through the property and down to the llama barn. Already out in the open air, enjoying the sunshine, Josie and Rico glanced up from a bale of hay as Paige and Jake approached. Josie went right back to eating, while Rico walked over to greet Paige.

"Rico, meet Jake…Jake, meet Rico," Paige said.

Jake frowned, watching Paige pet Rico's head. "I'm jealous," he admitted.

Paige smiled, moving her hand from Rico to Jake and petting Jake's head. "There," she laughed. "Is that better?"

Jake reached for Paige's arm and lowered it from his head. He took her other arm and held both arms gently, easing her back against the fence. Leaning forward, he kissed her and released her arms. She dropped them onto his shoulders and ran her fingers through his hair. Rico snorted and walked away.

"Much better," Jake whispered. "Now he's jealous."

"He has good reason to be." Paige smiled, drinking in the blue of Jake's eyes. *I can't get enough of this man...*

"Come back to Jackson Hole with me," Jake said suddenly.

"Wh..what?" Paige stuttered, taken aback. "I...can't, Jake. I have a job in New York. I can't just *not* go back."

"I know," Jake said, shaking his head. "I didn't plan to say that. And I don't mean for you to run away. But...think about it. If you moved to Jackson Hole, you could still write for *The Manhattan Post* as a correspondent. Maybe freelance for some other publications. Meanwhile, we could be closer to each other, spend more time together." He leaned closer, whispering in Paige's ear. "Get to know each other better..."

Paige's stomach did flip-flops. She was just adjusting to having their feelings verbalized, out in the open. Now he was suggesting she move to Jackson Hole.

"Just think about it, Paige," Jake said. "You could have your own place, still write, and still be as independent as you've always been..."

"And pig-headed?" Paige asked, raising her eyebrows.

"If you want," Jake laughed.

"And stubborn?" Paige continued.

"I think that goes without saying," Jake countered. "Just...think about it."

"OK," Paige said quietly. *Move to Jackson Hole?* "I'll think about it."

*   *   *   *

Paige closed the trunk of the rental car, her luggage packed away, ready for the drive to Albuquerque and her flight to New York. Her boarding pass was printed and tucked into her purse. A bottle of water sat in the car's drink

215

holder, a foil packet of *pan dulce* on the passenger seat. Luz and Marisol had insisted on packing up sweets for her trip.

"I'll be back in a minute; I just want to say thank you again," she said, heading back into the Agua Encantada office. She left Jake leaning against his own rental car, soaking in the New Mexico sun. He'd follow her to the airport, where they'd turn in both rental cars and board flights in different directions.

She'd said her good-byes to Luz and Marisol already. Luz had left for the store and Marisol had gone to the spa to check on Ana. Miguel had gone into town, but Paige was certain she'd caught a glimpse of his truck returning shortly before.

The lobby was subdued when she entered. Without any guests arriving until later that afternoon, the music was off and the lights, dim. In the silence, Paige took in the peaceful atmosphere and tucked it away in her memory. She would miss Agua Encantada and Tres Palomas, the physical beauty of the area, as well as the culture and, most of all, the people.

"Juanita sends her wishes for a safe trip home."

Paige had half expected and more than half hoped to hear this voice one last time. She whirled around to find Miguel leaning against the wall behind the open front door. Thumbs in his pockets, one foot against the wall, he looked exactly as he had the first time she'd met him – like a handsome New Mexico man, like trouble. Trouble she'd wisely avoided. She inhaled and exhaled slowly.

"You were not planning to leave without saying good-bye, were you?" Miguel shifted his weight, but remained against the wall. His cocky smile told Paige he already knew the answer: she would look for him before leaving. He motioned her toward him with one hand.

"Of course not." Paige took a step in his direction before stopping herself.

Miguel motioned again, succeeding in bringing Paige even closer, as if her legs moved of their own will.

"Promise me, Miguel," Paige said, "that you'll find someone special, someone who will make you happy."

"I will. Sometimes life is just timing." Miguel pushed away from the wall, just as he'd pushed away from the tree ten days before. But this time, instead of running his eyes the length of her body, he simply smiled and approached Paige, his brown eyes almost black in the dim light. For the second time in less than twenty-four hours, Paige felt the soft caress of fingers against her face and the warmth of a man's voice in her ear.

"Jake is a very lucky man," Miguel whispered, his lips barely grazing Paige's ear. "You take care of yourself, *Sonrisa*."

Paige held her breath as she listened to him walk away, followed by the sound of the back door closing. Slowly, she exhaled and replied to the empty room.

"You, too, Miguel."

CHAPTER THIRTY-THREE

Overhead speakers crackled and blared, a woman's voice filling the airport terminal. People shuffled by, briefcases and carry-on bags strapped over their shoulders, cell phones in their hands.

Flight Ninety-Seven boarding at Gate Fourteen.

"That's the second boarding call," Jake said. "You need to go."

"I don't want to." Paige pressed her head against Jake's chest, feeling the warmth of his arms around her. The two-hour drive in separate rental cars had given her plenty of time to think. She could hardly believe she'd been in a drug-laden storage shed not forty-eight hours before. She shuddered. So many things could have gone wrong that hadn't.

"You OK?" Jake asked, pulling back to look at Paige.

"Yes, just a little overwhelmed by everything. It's been a long ten days."

"Yes, it has," Jake agreed. He pulled Paige close, letting her rest against him once more, and kissed the top of her head. "I thought I'd lost you."

"You hadn't," Paige murmured.

"I would have blamed myself," Jake said, "for not telling you how I felt. That's why I came down here."

Paige sighed. "Are you sure it wasn't because you wanted to break into a warehouse? To help with a drug bust? To meet my boyfriend, Rico?"

"Well, yes," Jake said. "There was all that. Has anyone ever told you that life is never dull around you? Speaking of which, when *will* I be around you again?"

Paige lifted her head and stepped back, looking at Jake. So much was up in the air. "I don't know. I'll have to see when I get back to New York. I'll talk to Susan and see what options I have there."

"You'll think about my suggestion?" Jakes eyes held so much hope and yearning; Paige's heart came close to melting.

"Yes, I'll think about it," she said. "I'll think about it seriously. I just need some time to figure things out."

"Final boarding call for flight Ninety-Seven. Flight Ninety-Seven boarding at Gate Fourteen"

"That woman is getting really pushy," Paige said, frowning at the speakers and then back at Jake.

"Yes, she is," Jake agreed. "But she has other planes to get out of this airport, like mine, an hour from now. She has to be pushy." He reached down and lifted Paige's carry-on bag, walking her over to the gate.

"Ma'am, sir, the doors are about to close," an attendant said. "You need to finish your goodbyes."

"I'll call you when I get home." Paige said quickly, signaling to the attendant.

"When you get *home*?" Jake smiled.

"When I get to New York," Paige amended. With a quick kiss, she broke away and slipped through the gate just before the attendant closed it. Hurrying down the tunnel, she boarded the plane, found her window seat and stuffed her carry-on bag in the overhead compartment.

"Ladies and gentlemen, the captain has turned on the Fasten Seat Belt sign. If you haven't already done so, please stow your carry-on luggage underneath the seat in front of you or in an overhead bin. Please take your seat, fasten your seat belt and make sure your seat back and tray table are in their full upright and locked positions. At this time, we request that all electronic devices be turned off."

She sighed as she took her seat and followed the directions.

Leaning her head against the window, Paige watched as the plane pulled away from the terminal. Or, as it seemed, the terminal pulled away from the plane. A figure in the waiting area lifted an arm and waved. *Was it Jake?* She was too far away to tell, but she waved back, anyway.

She shifted her weight until she found a comfortable position and then leaned back against the seat and relaxed. Her mind wandered between varied memories she'd built during the last two weeks. Her arrival in New Mexico seemed so long ago, as did her initial impressions of Tres Palomas and its people – Luz, Marisol and Ana, at the resort, Whitehorse, Juanita, Abuela, Father John and the enigmatic Lena. Not to mention a variety of Gallup acquaintances she'd prefer to forget. And then there was Miguel.

To avoid obsessing about life's unexpected encounters, Paige pulled a magazine from the rack and flipped through the pages, but she was too full of recent experiences and too curious about those to come for her to be able to focus on anything else.

Paige adjusted her position once more as she felt the plane pick up speed. She cleared her mind and let the forward momentum press her back into the seat. As the plane lifted off the ground, she smiled. She wasn't sure what lay ahead, but for now that was all right. Wherever she was headed, it was into the future. And the future looked very promising, indeed.

ACKNOWLEDGEMENTS

An author gets credit for writing a book, but that's not entirely fair. So many people work behind the scenes and inside the scenes that I sometimes think all books should have a dozen or so co-author credits.

I owe thanks to Jay Garner and Paul Sterrett for their excellent plot suggestions throughout the story, as well as to Maggie Busto for giving Abuela's back story more substance. Carol Anderson's proofreading expertise always adds extra polish to a manuscript, no matter how "finished" it may seem to be. Special thanks go to Margarita Hernandez and Saul Sanchez for advising me on proper cuisine, culture and terminology to help bring a New Mexico story to life.

Not surprisingly, Elizabeth Christy has once again done an outstanding job as editor. Any manuscript that falls into her capable hands returns improved, tenfold. I'm so very fortunate to be able to work with her.

Keri Knutson, at Alchemy Book Covers, always does amazing work on cover art. And print and eBook formatting services, as usual, were expertly handled by Tim at Book Design and More, and Clare Ayala.

As always, I'm especially grateful for the constant support of family and friends. Their patience with me while I bounce back and forth between reality and imaginary worlds is not only impressive, but sincerely appreciated.

CPSIA information can be obtained
at www.ICGtesting.com
Printed in the USA
FSOW02n2122191115
13634FS